DEATHWIND

DEATHWIND

James Powell

DOUBLEDAY & COMPANY, INC.

GARDEN CITY, NEW YORK

1979

All the characters in this book are fictitious, and any resemblance to actual persons, living or dead, is purely coincidental.

ISBN: 0-385-14740-6
Library of Congress Catalog Card Number 78-14654

ONE

GHOST ON A SPOTTED MULE

1

The rider made no attempt to avoid the main road as he wound his way up the canyon toward Grafton. He could have easily enough; he could have stayed to the trees on the densely wooded north slope to his left, out of sight in the event other travelers should happen along. But none had, thus far, and Guthrie McGuire didn't really expect that any would. It was a cold, rapidly graying afternoon, the wind biting and cutting out of the north, and it was not an appealing day for traveling.

Not that it really mattered much to McGuire. He didn't think there was a soul alive in Grafton who would recognize him now. It had been well over two years since any of them had seen him. He wore a full beard in place of his once neatly trimmed mustache, and a straight-brimmed black hat pulled low over his eyes rather than the light gray Stetson he had once been known for; and he was a cowhand riding a mule instead of a cowpony—a paint mule at that, acquired in Socorro the day before. He was thinner now, too, and his face no longer carried the characteristic deep tan it always had before. He was a different man, this Guthrie McGuire. A dead man, actually. At least for now, to them . . .

So he stayed with the road, until he reached a point about a quarter of a mile below town where a dim trail led toward a heavy stand of oak brush. He reined the mule to a stop and for several moments simply sat there as if debating with himself whether or not to pass on by. A moment more and he turned the mule toward the oak stand. He knew what was on the other side, a place he must go, even if for just this one time. He had to see the grave, to make certain that at least they had buried her . . . at least that.

He found the cemetery on a small hill just beyond the oaks, looking much as he remembered it. There were more graves, of course; he had been gone almost half the place's lifetime, the earliest markers being dated late in 1880, the year of Grafton's settlement. But otherwise it looked much the same. The area was unfenced, so most graves and family plots had little protective fences of their own, mostly crude pickets encircling the plot, and markers varied from simple wooden crosses to, in a very few cases, expensive stones shipped in from no telling where. Spacing was irregular and without pattern, although some of the more recent entries were in a reasonable semblance of a row. Little paths wriggled variously among the graves, some obviously having been used regularly, some hardly at all. There were cut flowers on a few graves, but most of these were withered now from the recent cold, and on at least one or two clusters of what had been live blossoms before frost attested to careful planting and watering. Probably because there were no loved ones around to really care, most, on the other hand, looked neglected.

McGuire tied the mule to a bush, then began walking among the graves, studying the markers, searching for a certain one that he knew should be about a year old now—almost a year to the day, in fact. Except for the most recent, old and new were intermixed to the extent that he had to look at almost every one, at names most of which he did not recognize: three early-day miners killed by Apaches before he had come to Grafton, a couple of cowboys who had apparently shot each other less than six months back, two children of the same family who had died of smallpox in 1884

. . . names he did not know and graves he did not care about. He cared only for one.

When he found it, it looked pretty much as he had expected: no flowers, no expensive stone, no picket fence. Just a simple wooden marker stuck in the gravelly soil at the head of a dreadfully unimpressive little mound with weeds growing over it. And there was no glowing epitaph—hardly one at all, in fact. The crude markings on the board simply read:

CASSIE McGUIRE
Born: Date Unknown   Died: November 2, 1885
of Natural Causes

For a moment McGuire's throat became constricted and he had to fight back the tears that threatened to well up in his ordinarily hard brown eyes. Such a pitiful little bit to say about her . . . a woman, his wife, who had once been beautiful and happy and alive! They didn't even know her birth date. And to say she died of natural causes! The scum! Guthrie McGuire knew why she died. She had suffered from heartache, shame, despair—even from his prison cell over two hundred miles away he had learned that much. They had done it to her, those good people of Grafton; and it damn sure hadn't been natural. They had sent her husband off to jail, left her alone in the world with nobody to turn to, made her a whore, by God!

McGuire turned away sharply. The cold wind whipped about him and he turned his coat collar up to protect his neck and ears. Then he stared for a long several seconds up the canyon toward the town, as if debating once again. He had meant to go on around, once he had been to the cemetery. He had had that much caution about him, at least.

But now—now that he had seen the grave—renewed anger boiled up within him and a reckless arrogance replaced his caution. No one knew him now; he was supposed to be dead, mangled by a bear up near Las Vegas a month after his escape from prison. A deception born of careful design, just as was most of his changed appearance. And, by God, he thought, now is as good a time as any to stick it in their stupid damned faces, just to see. Just to by God see!

His jaw set, he returned to the mule—an oddly colored mare, chestnut with large white spots across her rump, her belly, and up one side of her neck and face—and walked around to the right side of the saddle. Carefully he drew the rifle from its scabbard, handling it as if it were a prized possession of some long-standing value. Which it was not; he had purchased it only a week earlier, in Albuquerque, and he wasn't even sure he liked it all that much.

A much-used .44 Winchester, it was essentially the 1860 model Henry, but with a side-gate loading mechanism, a heavy brass frame and butt plate, walnut half forestock, an upper sling swivel on the left side of the barrel and magazine tube, and using a .44-28-200 cartridge. He would have preferred something with a little more long-range accuracy, but it was what he could afford and he figured it would just have to do. He did not carry a sidearm, and for what he had in mind the knife at his belt was not likely to have much immediate use as a weapon. After a few moments he replaced the rifle in its scabbard, pulled the mule around, mounted, and turned the animal toward town.

He entered Main Street riding slowly, deliberately, paying little heed to the occasional curious pedestrian who stopped to stare at him before quickly moving on to get out of the cold. He stopped only once, just beyond Jeremy Chance's livery barn and the school and in front of Bay Calhoun's undertaking establishment (and Mrs. Calhoun's adjoining bakery), to stare across a broad-channeled arroyo to the south at the home of Clayton Usery. He knew Usery was still here and doing well, for that fact had been described to him in detail by the man who had sold him the mule in Socorro. Clayton Usery was well known, far and wide, and the size of his home reflected his prosperity. There were not many like it in places like Grafton, not many at all. McGuire was bitterly aware of that.

Presently he determined that no one was to be seen about the place and turned his attention back up the street. With cold mental efficiency, he noted details familiar and unfamiliar alike: Usery's General Store and post office, Wonderly's butcher shop, Celsa Jaramillo's dress shop, the Manor House Hotel and Restaurant, the California Saloon, the marshal's office and jail, an assay office, a laundry, a boot shop, three boardinghouses, a bank, Usery's Mining Company office, a stage company office, the town newspaper—all much as he remembered them. New, on the other hand, were at least two saloons, the Blake and the Pioneer, and at the far end—the other side of the arroyo where it cut across the canyon before loitering lazily down-canyon past the south side of town—stood what looked like a new church, probably Protestant, since across the road from it stood what McGuire knew to be a Catholic church that was almost as old as the town.

To the north, between the backs of the stores that fronted Main Street and a steep rocky bluff that effectively cut off development in that direction, things were about as always: a few scattered houses intermixed with barns, sheds, corrals, chicken pens, and dog pens. Across the arroyo to the south, however, several new houses had sprung up—some built of logs, others of planks or adobe—along the foot of the densely wooded ridge slope that bounded the town on that side of the canyon. Above town, to the west and beyond the churches, more new houses could be seen. Out of sight were the mines—the Silver Brick, the Glory Be, the Victorio—and beyond it all, in the distance to the west, the northernmost extreme of the Black Range Mountains reared skyward as they always had, a fine backdrop for such a thriving little town. . . .

But McGuire registered it as neither good nor bad that

the place had grown. It didn't matter to him. Like others of its ilk, Grafton would go as quickly as it had come, if and when the silver ever played out. Sure, it had become something of a small cattle town too, but that alone would never sustain it. Even now that the Apaches were no longer a real threat and people were easier to attract, there were other more centrally located towns in the vicinity that could serve the cattle interests better. McGuire cracked a humorless, bitter little smile as he thought about it. Poor Grafton, what misery it was destined to—and didn't even know it yet!

He spurred the mule lightly and continued on up the street, aware that his presence was creating some attention now. A stranger—any stranger—always stirred up interest in an out-of-the-way place like this. Especially one riding a paint mule straight through town as if he knew where he was going, acknowledging no one despite their stares. He even saw a couple of people he once knew: Celsa Jaramillo standing just outside the butcher shop and staring intently as the strange rider passed by—not out of recognition, apparently, just intense curiosity; and Quentin Usery, Clayton's no-good younger brother and partner in the various Usery enterprises around Grafton, preparing to mount a buckboard in front of the Pioneer Saloon. Again, there was no hint of recognition, only a dark look of wonderment as McGuire rode past.

He met only one rider coming into town from the west, a young, clear-eyed fellow wearing a sheepskin coat and riding a long-haired, long-legged grulla horse. McGuire rode by him without so much as a tip of his hat and did not look back as the other rider stopped to concentrate a penetrating gaze his way.

It bothered him a little, that gaze, for he could feel it at his back even when he could not see it. But that was all right. Let them wonder about him. They didn't know who he was, or where he was going, or when he would be back. They had been given a glimpse—of him, of what was to be—

and that was all the warning they would get. All they deserved.

Still without pause, he crossed the arroyo just below the new church—a Methodist church, he saw now by the sign out front—and seemingly vaporized a few moments later going upcanyon, in the trees and the darkening gray gloom of the afternoon.

2

The chill north wind sweeping down was not the first sign of a hard winter in Grafton that year; an early first frost, weeks before, had already foreboded harshness for the months ahead. How much so, or how widespread it would become, no one yet realized. But most sensed it spelled bad enough, and they knew there was snow in the air today. Maybe lots of it.

"Acting" Marshal Cal Sawyer numbered among these as he tied his grulla to the hitch rail in front of the town's small jail, and he fancied it no grand intuitive power that told him so. The massive black clouds to the north were rolling in fast now, and the cold was becoming bitter.

He opened the door of the jail, stepped inside with a "whoosh" of relief—and caught the jailer, one-legged old Enos Cooper, hobbling across the room with a stick of firewood in one hand and a crutch under the other arm, the already glowing hot fire inside the room's small black potbelly his obvious objective.

"'S 'bout time you got to town," he muttered, almost without looking up, and jammed the stick into the stove.

Cal smiled as he removed his hat and coat and hanged them on the rack beside the door. He had listened to old Enos' grouching and growling before, and he had learned better than to take it too seriously. He figured it was only human to be tolerant of the various temperaments of life's unfortunates, and Enos Cooper certainly fit that mold. A veteran of the Texas trail drives following the Civil War, a cowhand's cowhand, he had been foreman of Clayton Usery's Triple U ranch when an Apache bullet and an ensuing case of gangrene had cost him his right leg and ended his cowboying days forever. That had been two years ago, and probably because he so detested the charity and sympathy upon which he had become dependent, his disposition since had become one of almost constant irritability.

"I came in as soon as I could, Enos," Cal explained patiently, going over to the desk across the room. "You know I only took this as a part-time job. I told the committee that when I said I'd do it."

"Yeah, I know," the older man said sourly. He knew that Cal Sawyer had never claimed to be a lawman; he was a small rancher, a homesteader, a cowpuncher—hired solely on the basis that he had been about the only one around who needed the money bad enough to even consider the job. "Wasn't your fault Earl Youngblood let that damn miner beat hell out of him." Cal hadn't actually seen the fight but he knew it had been a bad one. It had happened over at the California Saloon on a wild Saturday night three days before, after which the miner had left town immediately, and the marshal, beaten terribly, had found himself lucky to be alive.

"Earl still over at the doc's house?" Cal asked as he fished around inside the top drawer of the desk for cigarette makings.

"Hell, I reckon!" Enos said with a disgusted look. "He's got busted ribs, a broke nose and cheekbone, a busted hand, screwed-up kidneys, insides all tore up, a back that hurts so bad he can't even sit up to eat . . . I never seen nobody so beat up before. Doc's sayin' now he'll be usin' a bedpan for another week and won't be fit to come back to work for a month—maybe longer."

This last statement came as something of a shock to Cal.

They had told him they thought a couple of weeks—which hadn't seemed so bad. But a month! And he had said he would stay on until Youngblood was well enough to return. He had not made the time period a condition for accepting the job at all. He could see now why Enos was concerned. "Believe me," he said, "I don't like this any better than you do. . . ."

But the other man waved this off impatiently. "It ain't you, damnit . . . nothin' the matter with you. Town just needs a full-time lawman is all. Been lucky we haven't had no more happen than we have since Earl got bunged up."

Cal sighed deeply. What Enos said was true. But for a couple of fist fights he'd heard about, Grafton had apparently been unusually quiet for the past three days, and it was the first time in a long time that the jail had no inmates to boast. It was also a situation that could hardly promise to last long—and it wasn't going to do for Cal to be at his ranch five miles from town when something did finally happen. Part-time or not, the job carried with it a responsibility, and not only was Cal no shirker, he also would have no one thinking he was.

At last locating tobacco and papers at the back of the desk drawer, he rolled his cigarette and lit it, then took a deep draw and let the smoke back out slowly. "Well," he said thoughtfully, "I suppose I've got things pretty well squared away around my place for a while. I sold my yearlings to Usery's foreman yesterday, and I finally got all my corn and hay in the barn for the winter today. Maybe I can stay around town full-time for a few days."

"That's good," Enos said as he hobbled over to a nearby chair and eased himself into it. "'Cause the weather don't look so hot out there—a good snow might even close the mines down. You know what that could do, I reckon."

Cal nodded grimly. "It'll put about a hundred miners in town all at once—too many of them in the saloons carousing it up to beat hell."

"That's right. And if they ain't controlled there'll be fights, knifin's, maybe shootin's even. Might not be much fun for you, boy."

Cal frowned. He was acutely aware of how rough a crowd those miners could be, had had little enough opportunity for him to forget what had happened to Earl Youngblood the last time the town marshal tried to stop a fight. He came to his feet and went over to the window, ostensibly to check conditions outside. After a few moments he suddenly turned and went to the coat rack.

"Where you goin' now?" Enos asked.

"Put my horse up over at Chance's, then to the hotel to get myself a room, and maybe over to the doc's to see Earl."

"You be comin' back here later?"

"Probably—after supper. I suppose I'll need to make a round to check the saloons, too."

"That'd be a good idea, all right," Enos said, as if that had been what was on his mind in the first place. "And the door locks up and down Main Street. 'Specially over at the Chinaman's eatin' place. Damn chink leaves it unlocked 'bout half the time. Can't remember nothin' no more, seems like."

"Anything else?" Cal asked, slightly impatient at all the instructions.

Enos started to wag his head, but then seemed to think of something. He withdrew an object from inside his shirt pocket and tossed it over to Cal. It was Earl Youngblood's badge. "Got that from the marshal this morning. Said he figured you'd be needin' it."

"Thanks a lot," Cal said.

"Go ahead—pin it on."

Cal reluctantly did as he was bidden. Then, as he was about to open the door to leave, he remembered something and turned momentarily back. "Say, you didn't happen to see a stranger ride through here on a spotted mule a while ago, did you?" he asked.

Enos gave him a puzzled look. "No. Don't reckon I did.

Don't reckon I ever seen nobody ridin' through here on a spotted mule before. Why?"

Cal shrugged. "I don't know for sure. Something about him, I guess. I just wondered if anyone had seen him before."

"You ask anybody else?"

"No. Not yet anyway."

"Might not be a bad idea, if the feller bothers you. Kinda thing a lawman'd do, I can tell you that."

"Yeah," Cal said, and went outside without another word.

3

Thoughts about the weather and the various problems associated with that so overshadowed any concern Cal might have had about the stranger on the paint mule that he forgot to ask Jeremy Chance over at the livery if he had seen them; and Cal had almost lost interest entirely by the time he obtained a room key at the hotel and then went next door to Doc Cleofus Wagner's house. The wind was colder than ever now, and a light sleet was already slanting down.

"You're worrying about a storm closing down the mines, I bet," Doc Wagner observed as he let Cal inside and pointed toward the nearest chair. "Oh I know . . . I saw you out there, staring at the sky like you'd lost your last friend. And I'd bet a gold piece it was that damnable Enos that set you to it, too."

"You don't think I should worry?"

The doc, a slender, gray-haired little man with a full beard and dark, bloodshot eyes, shrugged. "I know Enos," he said simply. "And I know it takes something special to close down even one shift at the Glory Be or the Silver Brick. Maybe not at the Victorio, because it's a small mine and isn't worked on much of a schedule anyway; but those other two belong to the Userys, and we both know they're not likely to lose a day's work, anytime they can help it."

Cal sighed. "I guess there's not much around Grafton that doesn't revolve around the Userys anymore, is there? Half the town's businesses, the two biggest mines, easily the biggest cattle outfit around. I'm surprised someone hasn't thought of changing the name to Useryville, or some such thing."

"Humph!" the doc grunted. "You're beginning to sound like Caleb Harvey now." Harvey was publisher, editor, and printer of the town's newspaper, the Grafton *Myriad*, and true to his breed, he had long ago made it clear that no one would be held an unfair target for his sometimes stinging editorials.

"What did he say now?" Cal asked, almost not wanting to find out.

"About the same thing you did—only stronger," the doc said. "Put it in yesterday's paper, he did. Even hinted that it'd be a more healthy situation if not so many of the town's citizens were beholden to one family for their livelihood; that maybe some new money and new blood wouldn't be a bad thing to have around here."

Cal wagged his head in amazement. "I'm surprised Clayt lets him get away with it."

The doc laughed. "Anybody else, he might not. It's Jenny, that pretty niece of Caleb's . . . and that damned Quentin trying to court her like she was the last girl left on earth. That's the main reason."

Cal kept his expression impassive, while inside he couldn't help feeling a sharp prick of annoyance. He had done little to hide his own interest in Jenny Bayles, even from the very day, two months ago, when she had come to Grafton to stay with her Uncle Caleb and Aunt Martha Harvey. He hadn't been doing too badly either. Twice now, he had been invited to take supper with the Harveys and Jenny; and once he had even escorted her to a Saturday night dance over at the school. He had been the envy of almost every single man in town . . . for a while . . . until Quentin had come along and begun to make his own serious effort to win the girl's hand.

Not that Cal couldn't stand the competition; he could. It was just that he wasn't certain how serious Quentin's intentions actually were. Easily fifteen years younger than Clayt, he was by the same token at least ten years Jenny's senior and was perfectly capable of trifling with her. Cal had heard how it had happened before with other girls around, and he suspected that Jenny had too—Caleb himself would have taken care of that. But in matters of the heart, Cal figured, no female could be held predictable. Not even Jenny . . .

Something about all of this must have shown on his face, for the doc said, "Damn me, Cal! I plain forgot you've been doing a little courting of your own over at the Harveys' place. I'm sorry as hell—"

"Forget it, Doc," Cal said uncomfortably. "It's not news to me that I've got a competitor."

"Yeah, well, just don't you give up on that damn Quentin's account, you hear?"

Cal didn't want to pursue the subject and he waved off further talk about it with an impatient little gesture. "Thanks, Doc. . . . I can't stay long. What I came for is to see how Earl's coming along."

The doc frowned. "He's still peein' blood and hurtin' inside to beat hell, if that's what you mean." Then he wagged his head, indicating some frustration. "I just wish I knew for sure if it's the ribs or something else that's causin' the pain. Not that there's much I can do about it, either way—'cept keep on givin' him laudanum and hopin' the pain lets up before he gets addicted to the stuff."

"Enos said it might be a month before he's well enough to come back to work."

The doc nodded. "I'm sorry, Cal . . . but for once old Enos didn't exaggerate. Looks like you're gonna have to hold down that marshal's post for at least that and probably longer."

Cal rose from his chair. "Well, I told them I'd do the job," he said resignedly.

"Did you want to see Earl?" the doc asked then. "He's fair-well doped up, but he's probably awake now."

Cal drew his watch from his pants pocket; it was almost five o'clock, time for Usery's shift wagons to be arriving in from the Glory Be and the Silver Brick. And through the window he could see that large, furiously wind-driven flakes of snow had replaced the sleet of a few minutes earlier.

He looked over at the doc and wagged his head. "I'd meant to. But maybe I'd best let it wait till tomorrow. The shifts at the mines have changed and there'll be a few of those fellows hitting the saloons pretty soon. I'd like to take supper and then amble around town a bit—sort of keep an eye on how things are going."

The doc seemed to understand, for he said, "Usually along about midmorning's a better time to visit Earl, anyhow, I reckon. Maybe you can make it then."

"I'll plan on it," Cal promised as he stepped to the door. "Thanks, Doc."

Outside, the snow and wind so blasted him that he was shocked by their combined intensity. Across the street, in front of the general store, the first shift wagon was just pulling up—not coincidentally across from the Usery-owned Pioneer Saloon, which was immediately next door to Doc Wagner's house. The wagon was only half full, since many of the miners lived above town and had already been let off; of those remaining, about half were already on their way toward the Pioneer, two or three others were trudging toward Roque Gutierrez's California Saloon, set diagonally across on the next block, and the rest appeared headed toward their individual places of residence, which, for most, was one or the other of the three different boardinghouses located on or near Main Street. Farther up the street, having just crossed the bridge below the churches, came the second shift wagon, and Cal knew a third would not be far behind that.

He stood there in the cold for several moments, staring toward the saloons and watching the shift wagons. Then, finally, figuring it would be yet another hour or so before he needed to worry about patrolling the streets in earnest, he turned toward the hotel restaurant next door. As he went, he felt a strange sense of weightiness about his person, characterized in one instance by the Colt revolver at his hip, which he was unaccustomed to wearing, and in another by the badge on his shirt, which certainly felt much heavier than its own physical structure could ever merit. But there was also something else . . . something not physical at all. It was an irrepressible uneasiness that he somehow doubted could have been spawned by even a herd of rowdy miners crowding the town's saloons.

4

The rider sat and watched from within a dense brush motte that was protection both from the wind and snow and the eyes of others. He had been there for almost an hour now, and he had been watching the small, poorly constructed log cabin that was the last house going upcanyon toward the mines. It belonged to a pair of bachelor brothers named Jess and Hiram La Belle—at least he hoped it still did. Already he had watched two shift wagons pass by without letting anybody off.

He was just about to give up, to decide the La Belles no longer lived there, or no longer worked at the mines—or maybe had been aboard one of the first two shift wagons but were going on into town for something—when suddenly the third wagon appeared, coming down the canyon from the direction of the Glory Be. He watched intently as the wagon stopped on the road fifty yards below the cabin. He watched even more intently as two figures dismounted and began tramping against the cold wind and snow up the low hill on which the cabin sat.

They were the La Belles, all right; even from this distance and through the heavy swirl of snowflakes, he could tell. He remembered them as plainly as if it had been yesterday: Jess, thin and dark, his thick black hair beginning to gray, his face narrow and hawklike with a thin mustache that just darkened his upper lip; Hiram, on the other hand, blocky of build and fair of skin, a balding head and a full beard, and a good three inches shorter.

So physically unalike they were totally distinctive, no one would even guess they were brothers. But McGuire knew them well enough to know who they were. He knew they had lived in Grafton almost since its inception; that they had prospected almost every hillside and canyon bottom around within the first year after they arrived; that they had, to give them credit, helped fight off more than one Indian attack; that they had gone to work for the Usery Mining Company almost four years ago and had apparently worked for it ever since. He knew all of this about them and more. But most of all, he knew them for what they had done to him, how, a few years back, they not only shared the lead in the posse that tracked him down and brought him back to face trial for cattle rustling, but had testified against him to boot. He remembered this very, very well.

His eyes never wavered as the twosome mounted the front porch of the cabin and stomped their feet in a useless attempt to clean the snow and mud from them before going inside. He watched grimly as they closed the door behind themselves and disappeared. And he told himself that one or both would probably come back out for something or another in a while; that he would still be waiting when they did. . . .

He stepped down from the mule, noting not for the first

time that the La Belles' cabin was over two hundred yards from its nearest neighbor and thinking that little sound, if any, would carry that far over the howling of the wind and the mounting thickness of the snow. Calmly, he reached across the saddle and withdrew the Winchester from its scabbard.

TWO

DEAD MEN IN THE SNOW

1

The storm blew itself out sometime before daybreak, leaving behind eight inches of snow, a clear blue sky, and a morning stillness that was unbelievably cold. But it was neither this nor the blinding white brilliance of the scene below that riveted Cal Sawyer's attention as he looked down on things from his room at the hotel an hour past sunup. He was looking at the wheel tracks of the shift wagons that had already gone up Main Street toward the mines; wondering if he really should be so relieved that the Userys had indeed decided not to close down the mines, and marveling at the same time that even they thought much work could be done under such conditions as these.

In any event, he told himself, the shift wagons had gone out—at least one or two of them—and it suited him just fine that they had. He had counted himself lucky the previous evening when things had proven even calmer than usual around the saloons, but he was in no way willing to depend on that remaining the case the minute those miners had a day off. He didn't like the idea that he might be becoming a little bit paranoid about it, either; but he figured he needed as few things going against him as possible, and those miners staying at the mines and not in the saloons was a help, to say the least.

He was still thinking this a few minutes later as he en-

tered the dining hall downstairs and he almost didn't notice
Cora Usery, Clayt's wife and patroness of the Manor
House Restaurant, smile at him from across the room. As she
came his way he seated himself at a table near the door, noticing at the same time that there were only a couple of
other customers at the moment, seated together two tables
away.

"Well, if it isn't our handsome young town marshal!" Cora
greeted brightly. "You look sort of preoccupied this morning, Cal."

She was hardly any older than Cal himself, and was very
pretty. Usery, a widower, had met her on a business trip to
San Francisco a year ago and had married her following
what most folks figured must have been a whirlwind ro-
mance of the grandest proportions. As in his first marriage,
however, the union had thus far been childless, and Cora
hardly seemed the type to sit around any man's house with
nothing to do but order her servants around. No one seemed
to know much about her background—although in a western
town that wasn't really necessary anyway—but she was
plainly young and vivacious . . . and maybe, some thought,
just a little more than a man twice her age was meant to
handle.

Regardless of this—or maybe because of it—Clayt had allowed her to take on the job of running the hotel's eating establishment, and she wasn't doing a bad job of it at all. Fact
was, she had already cut into the Chinaman's business down
the street, and that had to be something Clayton Usery
liked.

"I guess I have been a little preoccupied, all right," he
said finally. "Seems like I took on a bit more than I thought
I did with this town marshal business."

She seemed surprised, but mostly as if she had not
thought about it before. "Have you been having trouble?"

"It's not that—at least not yet, anyway. In fact, last night
was so quiet I almost couldn't believe it. It's just that I don't

know how long it will last, and it definitely looks like I've got the job for longer than I'd figured on."

"Oh?"

"The doc's saying Earl may be laid up for as much as a month or more now. When I talked to the committee, they seemed to think two weeks at the most . . . though I suppose it's as much as they knew at the time. Even Doc probably didn't know yet."

She didn't say anything to this, just looked thoughtful. "Anyway," Cal went on, "I'm not crying about it. I'll do what I said I'd do."

She smiled. "That's the spirit! Can I get you something for breakfast? Might as well—the committee's paying for it, you know."

He had almost forgotten, but that had been part of the bargain: meals and lodging free whenever he had to stay in town . . . as long as both expenses were kept within reason, of course.

"We've got fresh sourdough biscuits and honey," Cora was telling him. "Eggs, smoke-cured ham brought over from Wonderly's last night, steak . . ."

"Ham and eggs sounds great." He hardly had to hesitate at the choice. "And the biscuits and honey too. No way I can eat like that very often out at my place."

"Coming right up," she said and headed for the kitchen.

In no time she was back with a steaming cup of coffee, and a few minutes after that with his food. Then, after the other two customers had paid for their meals and left, she brought over a coffee pot and a cup for herself. "You don't mind my company, I hope?"

"Not at all," he said as she took a chair across the table from him. "Guess business is a little slow this morning."

She shrugged lightly. "A little, maybe. But it usually slows down about now, anyway. We normally have quite a few in here before the shift wagons go out, then a few stragglers like you up until about eight or eight-thirty. After that there usually isn't much doing until noon. Gets a little boring, actually."

"Yeah. I suppose it would," he said, finishing up his ham and eggs and pouring honey over the last biscuit. "I was a little surprised the shift wagons went out today."

She gave him an undecipherable little look, then answered, "You know Clayt and Quentin better than that, Cal. Where there's silver to come out of the ground, nothing stands in their way. 'Two shifts a day, six days a week'— that's the motto." She made very little effort to hide the fact that she wasn't entirely happy with the circumstance, either.

"Well, I suppose that's the way businesses are run," he said simply, finishing up the biscuit and reaching for his coffee cup. "I guess Clayt and Quentin do stay pretty busy these days. I know I don't see them around town much anymore."

"You see them almost as much as I do, I imagine," she observed with a sort of wistful little smile. "Quentin's been at the mines most of the time, and Clayt's either there or at the ranch, or at the store . . . or at the house when I'm here. . . ."

She had added this last almost as if not meaning to, and Cal couldn't help a puzzled look over it.

"It's no big deal, Cal," she explained, seeing his expression. "Clayt has been gone at the ranch nights so much lately that I simply decided to start staying at the hotel instead of going home. It's lonely out there, even with Juanita and Carlos over in the east wing, and it saves me that cold morning walk it takes to get here in time for breakfast." She shrugged. "So . . . we've agreed this would be better. It's as simple as that."

Somehow Cal doubted if it really was all that simple. Certainly, Clayt Usery's rambling, U-shaped adobe home was too spacious for one person alone not to become lonely at night, especially a woman. But that the man was spending so many nights out at the ranch that his wife found it more inviting at the hotel just did not make sense to Cal. "Will Clayt be in town today?" he asked after the moment. "I'd sort of thought I might look him up about this part-time job of mine if I got the chance."

Again she shrugged. "He was at the ranch yesterday. But he's usually in town on Wednesdays. . . . In fact, he usually comes in early and stops by for coffee." She looked around then. "Do you want some more coffee?"

He hesitated, wondering if he shouldn't be getting on over to the office, though knowing there probably wouldn't be all that much to do there anyway. And he did need to see Clayt. "Well," he said finally, "maybe one more cup."

She poured his cup full, then asked, "Are you really that concerned about being town marshal for a month, Cal?"

He managed a sheepish smile. "I guess I do sound like a big worry wart over it, don't I?"

She studied him for a moment. "No," she said, "I don't think you sound that way at all. I think you simply want to do your job right, and you're worried about being able to."

He gave her a grateful look. "I'm not sure that's any different than what I said, but it's a kinder way to put it, at least."

She seemed about to respond to this with some rather earnest protestation when she saw something over Cal's shoulder and stopped. Cal turned to see Clayton Usery standing in the doorway, a slight frown on his face. He hesitated only a moment that way before replacing it with a somewhat more pleasant expression, then stepped over to their table.

"Morning, Clayt," Cal said, rising and putting out a hand. "I've been sort of waiting around for you to show up."

Usery accepted the handshake with a solid grip. He was not a particularly big man—slightly less than Cal's own six-foot height—but he was square-shouldered and quite strong. Cal didn't know the man's exact age, but he was certain it had to be at least the early fifties. His hair was dark, gray-streaked, and full; he wore his sideburns full and low, al-

most to the point of his jaw, and his mustache swept down
to connect with them in the currently popular fashion. He
had obviously just come in from outside, probably the
ranch, for he wore work clothes—sheepskin coat, overalls,
chaps, a heavy plaid shirt, and carried a sweat-rimmed hat
and gloves in his left hand. He did not wear a sidearm, at
least not on his outer person, although Cal would not have
been surprised to know that he concealed a small pistol or
derringer in a coat or chaps pocket.

"You could've had a long wait," he said, in reply to Cal's
remark. "I almost didn't come in at all. Snow's drifted deep
as two–three feet in some places. Tough as hell on a horse,
let me tell you!" He shed his sheepskin coat and pulled up a
chair, and only after·he was already seated did he seem to
take notice of his wife.

"I was just keeping Cal company while he was having
breakfast," she explained.

"I can see that," he said somewhat tersely, almost without
looking at her.

Cal wasn't sure, but he thought she winced slightly under
the remark. But she only said, "Do you want breakfast?"

He shook his head. "Just coffee. I ate at the ranch before
sunup." She brought him a cup, poured it full, then picked
up Cal's plate and disappeared through the kitchen bat-
wings. She apparently considered herself dismissed, for she
did not come back out.

Usery looked over at Cal. "Well, you were waiting to see
me. What about?"

Cal, having become somewhat intrigued by the byplay
between man and wife, started slightly. "Have you talked
with Doc since you last saw me? About Earl?"

"How do you mean?"

"Doc says a month at least before Earl's back on the job."

Usery sighed. "And we told you two weeks at the most.
Well, I guess I have to apologize for that, Cal. That's what
Doc thought at the time, though admittedly it was an esti-

mate he didn't want to make so soon. In any event, we hired you and we'll pay you for as long as Earl's laid up—if you'll stay on that long."

"That's just it," Cal said. "I'm no lawman, Clayt. You know that as well as I do. And this town is no cinch for someone like me to control. Sure, maybe for a couple of weeks, if all goes right. But for a month or more . . . well, I just want you to know I can make no promises. . . ."

"Do you want out?" Usery asked abruptly. "Is that what you want? You know we couldn't find anybody else—"

"And I know why, too," Cal inserted meaningfully. "One look at what happened to Earl Youngblood is enough to discourage anybody with any sense at all. But no, I'm not asking to get out. I'll try if you want me to. I only ask two things."

"Which are?" Usery's eyes narrowed.

"One is the miners. They are the ones who cause most of the trouble around here. And most of them work for you. I want it understood that none will receive any special quarter if they break the law or cause trouble of any kind in or around Grafton. I want it known that things will go damn tough on any who even try."

Usery's eyes remained narrowed and noncommittal. "And the second thing?"

"I'll only stay on the job until Earl Youngblood comes back, or a month—whichever comes first. If Earl isn't back to work by then, or if he decides never to come back, you'll have to find someone else. I have my own place to take care of, and I don't want this deal to drag on into a permanent obligation."

"What do you mean, 'if Earl decides never to come back'?" Usery asked pointedly, apparently having caught onto this as a bit of perception that should intrigue him keenly. "Did Doc tell you something he didn't me?"

Cal shook his head. "No, I don't think so. But I've been thinking about what it would be like for Earl, after what's happened to him. A man has to have the upper hand to keep control of a bunch of rowdy miners. He can't whip them all and he never could, but he does have to have the bluff on them. Earl's been whipped and he's been whipped good, and I think it'll occur to him sooner or later that every miner in this town is going to know that. I'm not sure he'll want the job anymore, and if he does, I'm not sure he'll be able to hold it. If he doesn't want it, for sure you'll be having to find another man. And that damn sure won't be me!"

It was Usery's turn to shake his head. "Don't you think you're exaggerating just a bit, Cal? I know this town's not the easiest to ride herd on, but I don't think it's all that bad, either. Sure, a fist fight now and then, and, I admit, a knife- or gunfight occasionally. But that's the way with any western town. These men work hard and they drink hard. Few of them have a woman or any contact with women. They're tough because they live in a man's world. But I think you'll be able to handle them, and so will Earl when he's healed up and all."

"But you agree to my conditions," Cal said, not conceding the point but choosing not to argue it further. "I can't do the job for you any other way."

Usery sighed. "Yes . . . I agree. I'll tell the committee how it is, and I'll back you up if you have trouble. But we will expect you to stay on at least as long as you said. You agree to that, of course."

"Yes. I'll stay on that long."

Usery pulled a watch from his shirt pocket and looked around as if for Cora. She was still nowhere to be seen. "Well," he said resignedly, "I've got to be getting over to the store, then out to the Glory Be. This damn snow will be playing hell with the work out there."

They both stood up, Cal leaving a tip for Cora on the table, and then headed for the door together. Usery was saying, "Don't you be worrying about keeping order around town, Cal. You'll be surprised how little trouble there really is. . . ."

It was then that the driver of one of the shift wagons that had gone out earlier came bursting into the lobby of the hotel. He had been looking all over town for Cal. He and some others had just a little while ago found the La Belle brothers, outside their cabin above town, shot dead in the snow.

2

Cal and Usery, having dispatched the shift wagon driver to hunt up the undertaker, rode in the wheel ruts of the shift wagons all the way to the La Belle cabin. They dismounted before a small knot of men standing in front of the cabin. A shift wagon sat nearby, its team of four horses stamping their feet and blowing lungfuls of frosty breath into the air. It was this wagon, the third, that the La Belles always rode to and from the mines.

One of the group of men, a worker at the Glory Be Mine, came forward. His name was Salvador Gonzales. "The bodies are around back, Señor Usery. There was trouble with the wagon and it was late getting here. The La Belles were not waiting beside the road as they usually are, so we came looking for them. . . . We found them both dead."

They followed Gonzales over a trail beaten out through drifted snow, around the cabin almost to the back. They came upon Hiram's body first. It was grotesquely slumped against the corner of the house, frozen almost stiff. He had been shot twice, once through the shoulder, once through the chest. He clutched a lever-action rifle as if he had been running, carrying it across his chest like an infantry soldier in the midst of a charge. A few yards farther, within twenty feet of a flimsy, snow-covered outhouse, lay the body of Jess. He had been shot only once, through the neck, his jugular severed and now-frozen blood covering the upper torso. Neither body had been moved, according to Gonzales, but both had been almost completely blanketed with snow when found, and that had been swept away.

Cal, noting carefully the positions of the bodies, asked Gonzales, "You're sure no one moved them?"

"Sí, I am sure. I have been here all the time. I made sure no one did a thing, except sweep away the snow."

"And when you first got here . . . was there any sign of tracks? Any at all?"

"None, señor. I remember plainly how very white it looked. And smooth, almost perfectly smooth, except where the wind had caused drifts to ripple the surface. That is why I saw so quick Señor Hiram's head and shoulders sticking up over there, and then Señor Jess's hand and arm over here."

Cal thought for a moment, then walked to each body in turn. Almost without knowing why at first, he studied the way each had fallen, then the direction each must have been facing when hit and the side on which the bullets had entered. He came back to stand beside Usery. "I think these men were shot from some distance away, Clayt. Probably from off to the right there . . ." His eyes settled on an oak clump at the foot of the ridge. After a moment, he turned back to Gonzales. "Did these men work at the mines yesterday? Did they ride the shift wagon in yesterday afternoon?"

"Sí. Just like always. The third wagon, right along with myself and these other men here."

"Then they were shot sometime after it started snowing . . . but before enough had fallen to cover them, which means it had to be between five and six o'clock, right in the middle of the storm. Before dark, too, or whoever did it wouldn't have been able to see. . . ."

"Pretty good shooting, in a snowstorm," Usery put in, his eyes on the same oak clump Cal had observed. "But tell me why in hell no one heard the shots. That's what I want to know."

Cal looked toward the nearest house. "Probably the storm," he said, trying to picture it. "Unless maybe someone *did* hear. Three shots at least, probably fired not too far apart: Jess shot first while he was on his way to the outhouse, and Hiram hearing and coming on the run. . . . Salvador, whose house is that down there?"

"It is an empty house, *señor*. No one has lived there for over two months."

"Figures," Cal said glumly. "How about the one just beyond it? Anyone live there?"

Gonzales suddenly looked sheepish. "That is my house, *señor*. I live there with my wife and two little sons. . . . I am afraid we heard nothing. At least I did not, and I do not think my wife did either."

Cal met a look from Usery. "I guess it's pretty certain no one saw anything either." Back to Gonzales, he asked, "How about the cabin? Did you go inside?"

Gonzales nodded. "The door was open and snow had blown all over. Señor Hiram must have left it that way. We only went in to find a broom to sweep away the snow—"

"Was anything disturbed? Did it look as if someone had searched it, maybe for something to steal?"

"Not that I could tell, *señor*. It looked like someone was fixing a meal—a frying pan on the stove, some venison steaks and a butcher knife on the table . . . but that's all. Nothing looked disturbed."

Cal, puzzled, turned to Usery. "Do you know of anybody holding a grudge against the La Belles? Any reason at all someone would shoot them down in cold blood like this?"

"None," Usery said flatly. "Absolutely none. These were good men, Cal. They were hard workers, and I never knew them to cause trouble. They kept to themselves mostly. I cannot think of a reason in the world for this. No reason at all."

"I cannot either, *señor*," Gonzales offered as Cal looked once again his way. "I know of no one."

For several seconds Cal simply stood there surveying the scene around him and wondering what more he could ask or do. He even tried to imagine what Earl Youngblood would have done, but quickly decided that that would probably be no more than he himself already had. Of course, this thought did present him one possibility: He could go talk to Earl, which certainly couldn't hurt anything and might even help.

He turned to Usery. "Well—any suggestions?"

Usery shook his head. "I'm stumped, Cal. I don't know what to say."

"Do you think I should get word to the county sheriff in Socorro?"

"Tom Rudabaugh?" Usery raised his eyebrows slightly. "Yes . . . I suppose we should let Tom know. But don't count on him coming up here to help. You know how it is with him. Socorro itself is enough trouble—let the mining towns take care of their own problems. Can't say I blame him much, either. It's seventy-five miles almost any way you go to get here from there, a hundred or better by road. Fact is, last time I remember seeing old Tom in Grafton was when he came to escort Guthrie McGuire to Socorro for trial —and that was two years ago. . . ." His words trailed off as if the memory had brought something back he had not thought about—or had not wanted to—for some time.

"McGuire," Cal said, rolling the name across his tongue thoughtfully. "I've heard that name, although this trial you're talking about had to be before my time. There was a woman, wasn't there? A woman named McGuire. I remember hearing about her because she died only a few weeks before I came here."

A strange look came into Usery's eyes upon Cal's mention of the woman, a suspicious, penetrating look that seemed to ask if Cal knew more than he had let on. Then, quickly, it passed, and Usery said, "Cassie. Cassie McGuire. She was the man's wife . . . stayed here even after he was gone."

"What happened to him? Is he in prison?"

"He was, in Santa Fe . . . until a few months ago. Seems he busted out, then was killed by a bear or something up near Las Vegas. Someone read it in a Santa Fe newspaper. It was good riddance, too, I reckon. The man was a bad one, a damn bad one." His tone seemed to dismiss the subject; yet still there was the strange look in his eyes, and because of it Cal found it strangely difficult to let the subject drop.

Nevertheless, he said, "Well, anyway, I'll get word to Rudabaugh about this. Maybe he'll have an idea or two that we don't."

"And then what?" Usery asked. "Have you any other plans?"

Cal shrugged. "I'm not sure. Right now I guess I'll poke around inside the cabin a bit—just in case Salvador missed something. Then maybe I'll plow over to that oak clump. Probably won't find anything now that the snow's covered things over, but it can't hurt to try, I guess. Beyond that, I just don't know—except maybe ask around town, see if anyone else can think of a reason for this. Maybe Earl Youngblood will know something. . . ."

Usery, who had not been quite the same since the mention of the McGuire woman, stared rather soberly at the snow for a few moments, then sighed and straightened. "Yes. That's a good idea. Check with Earl." And with a sweeping glance past the two dead men, he turned to look back down the canyon where, on the road from town, Bay Calhoun's undertaking wagon had just come into view.

3

Cal watched a short while later as Calhoun's wagon rolled slowly back down the road toward town, slipping and sliding in its own ruts as it went. There seemed little danger that the road would soon thaw sufficiently underneath to make it impassable, however, and on that basis the shift wagon had also departed, several minutes earlier, on its way to the mines, with Clayton Usery riding alongside. Which left Cal alone, hardly comfortable with his thoughts but confident there was little else he could do where he was.

Nevertheless, he still did not leave, stubbornly disbelieving that there were just no clues at all to be found. But even stubbornness has its limits, and after a while he was finally forced to admit that he might as well give up. He had found no sign of anything remiss inside the cabin, and stomping back and forth between where the bodies had been found and the oak motte where he suspected the killer might have been concealed had proven futile at best. Maybe when the snow melted he might find some sign—a shell casing lying on the ground, a footprint frozen beneath the snow—but not now, not today. And even then, what would things like that prove?

He shook his head. All he knew was that two men had been killed, and he hadn't an idea under the sun who had done it. Worse, he had even less idea how to find out. That was what bothered him most just then, the inadequacy he felt, the fact that he was so unsure what to do next.

Yet maybe that's a foolish way to look at it, he told himself as he made sure the door to the cabin was fast shut and then went over to where his horse was tied. What would anyone else—including an experienced lawman—know to do about a deal like this? What would a sheriff or a marshal do, faced with the same problem? He would find a place to start, wouldn't he? Nothing more, nothing less. He would find a place to start. . . .

And go from there.

THREE

SO LITTLE TO GO ON

1

Cal rode into town with the intention of going straight to Doc Wagner's house and Earl Youngblood, then to the post office to get off a letter to Tom Rudabaugh in Socorro, for there was no telegraph line between the two towns, and the stage—which carried the mail—was due to make a run to the county seat tomorrow. Thus, short of sending a rider out today (and he had no idea who that would be), the mail was probably as fast a way as any to get word to Rudabaugh. And Cal wanted every bit of help he could get from a real lawman.

But almost the minute he reached town, he realized that first things were not necessarily going to come first. He got no farther than the bank before he was hailed by a small group of men who had been standing there, talking earnestly among themselves when they saw Cal coming down the street. The group included Little Mike Wonderly, Roque Gutierrez, Jeremy Chance, and Usery's bank manager, Mel Cole. It was Wonderly who called Cal over.

"You gotta tell us what's going on, Cal," he said. He was a smallish man, barely five feet tall and light of frame, was clean-shaven, and had as a trademark the habit of rarely, if ever, wearing a hat. "This town's been nothing but a heart-stop since we heard there was a shooting up at the La Belles' cabin last night. Is it true? Are they both dead?"

Cal pulled up at the boardwalk but did not dismount. He looked down on the four men. "I'm afraid so, Mike. Shot from ambush, apparently. By who—or why—we have no idea."

The men on the boardwalk exchanged expressions of appall and dismay. Not that any of them were easily shocked by news of violence from this raw, wild land in which they lived; they were not. But the apparent cold-bloodedness of this—two murders without clear reason or suspect—was enough to cause concern and uncertainty among the best of men.

Jeremy Chance, a wiry fellow only a few inches taller than Wonderly and who looked anything but the blacksmith he was, shook his head. "Just like that," he murmured. He had reddish-blond hair, a straight, well-kept mustache, and hazel eyes that bugged slightly and looked much too large for his narrow face. Right now they looked even bigger than usual. "No sign of *anybody?*"

Cal's answer was a somber look and a clipped, "None." He went on, however, to relate all that he knew or had guessed so far, and to ask if any of the four men could think of anything that would provide a clue as to someone with a motive for the killings.

"You think robbery is out?" Banker Cole asked. "Did you search the bodies to see if they had any money left on them?"

Cal had to admit he hadn't even thought of that, an oversight he would have to correct as soon as he could make it over to Calhoun's mortuary. But even then he doubted he would learn anything new. "I just don't think robbery was the reason, Mel. The bodies didn't look as if they had been touched, and there was no sign of any disturbance inside the house. I think they were shot down and left lay by someone who simply wanted them dead and nothing else."

Only Roque Gutierrez had remained silent throughout, and Cal's eyes turned toward him inquiringly. A tall, dark

Spaniard whom Cal knew only casually, the owner of the California Saloon returned the look with a concerned frown. He seemed half lost in thought, almost as if he were not going to reply at all. But then, finally, he did say, "I know of no one, *señor*. The La Belles never caused trouble; they seldom showed their faces in my saloon and I don't think they were seen much more in the Blake or the Pioneer. Unless there was some trouble at the mines . . . someone they worked with there . . ."

Cal shook his head dubiously. "I asked Sal Gonzales and Clayt Usery both, and they couldn't think of anything like that."

"It is all I can think of, *señor*," Gutierrez said. "Unless maybe . . ." Again he looked thoughtful, then unsure.

"What is it?"

The thoughtful look passed and it was the Spaniard's turn to shake his head. "Nothing. An impossibility. I would not even repeat it."

"Well," Cal said resignedly, "if any of you do think of something, let me know. Okay?"

Leaving them standing there, he rode on up the street to the doc's house and found Earl Youngblood sitting up in bed, looking bad but claiming to feel better than he had any day since the fight.

"Have you heard what happened?" Cal asked, taking a seat beside the bed.

The marshal's craggy, lean face still showed signs of the beating he had received—a cut over one eye, nose and one cheek horribly misshapen, bruises and splotches from forehead to chin—but his deep-set brown eyes were steady and direct through their pain.

He said, "The doc told me just a bit ago. You know who did it?"

"Don't even have a clue," Cal said unhappily. "No motive, nothing."

"They weren't robbed? Nothing was stolen?"

"Not that I've been able to detect."

Youngblood frowned. "So now you don't know what to do next. That right?"

"Pretty much. Except I figured I'd ask around, hoping I'd finally run across someone with an idea who might hold some sort of grudge against the La Belles . . . something at least to go on. Which seems like a pretty far-out hope right now to me."

"I know plenty of lawmen who haven't even had that," Youngblood said flatly.

Somehow Cal wasn't comforted. He only frowned.

"Have you done anything to let Tom Rudabaugh in Socorro know about this?" Youngblood went on to ask.

Cal shook his head. "I plan to, though. Just as soon as I leave here. Clayt Usery said Rudabaugh wasn't likely to rush up here to help, but we decided it wouldn't hurt to try anyhow."

Youngblood shrugged. "Maybe he'll come, maybe he won't. You never can tell about Tom. But you oughta let him know. That'd be the first thing to do, in a case like this."

"But then what?" Cal asked earnestly. "What's the next step? What would *you* do?"

Youngblood gave him a somewhat vacant stare. "What would I do?" He repeated it almost absently, looking down at himself as he lay there helplessly abed, weak and hurt and probably feeling very old, much more so than he should have.

He let his eyes come back to meet Cal's, frustration and impotence showing starkly in them. "What would I do? Who in hell am I to say what oughta be done! Look at me! Whupped to beat hell by a no-account miner whose name I don't even remember. Helpless as a goddamn baby . . ."

Cal tried to be comforting. "It could have happened to anyone, Earl. You know that."

"*Anyone!* Hell yes, anyone!" the older man blustered. "But not to the man that wants to be marshal of this town.

No way that, young man!" There was a moistness in his eyes, a knowledge that Cal had predicted might come but hated to see. Earl Youngblood was neither a weak nor a defeated man—at least not in the larger sense—but he was not a stupid man, either; he would never again be marshal of Grafton, and he knew it.

"I'm sorry, Earl," Cal said.

The marshal waved this off with a weak hand. "It's not your fault, boy. You came here for help and I'm not giving you any. It's just that there is no magic thing to do, no step-by-step procedure. You keep your ears open and your eyes peeled. You ask all the questions that can be asked, and look everywhere. And you let time pass as it will. You may find what you're looking for and you may not. I'm sorry, but that's all I know to tell you."

"You know of no reason anyone would want to kill those two men?"

Youngblood shook his head. "A few years ago—hell, even a year ago—I'd have thought maybe Apaches. They don't need no special reason for wanting to kill a white man. But not now. Not since they've all been hounded out of this part of the country and put on reservations—all but a few still hanging on down in Mexico and maybe a renegade or two here and there. Possible, I suppose, but not likely. And who else might have done it . . . I just don't know."

Cal hesitated a moment, then said, "There was a man named McGuire, a cattle rustler caught and sent off to jail a couple or three years back. Clayt Usery mentioned him to me."

Youngblood's eyes narrowed instantly. "What about McGuire, boy? What'd Usery tell you?"

"Nothing much. Except he left a wife who died a year ago. I knew about her but not about McGuire himself. Clayt said the man was dead now, but—"

"But what? A dead man's a dead man. And he's right: that's exactly what McGuire is. I heard about it, too. A bear mauled him up near Las Vegas after he'd broke jail in Santa Fe. Ain't no way McGuire could've had anything to do with this."

"Except he could have held a grudge against someone in this town. Did the La Belles have anything to do with McGuire, Earl?"

Youngblood harrumphed. "Not much, I don't reckon." Then he frowned. "'Cept they may have been in the posse that brought him in. Yeah, I believe that's possible, all right. And there was something at the trial . . . but don't matter none. The man's dead, I tell you."

Cal remembered then the stranger who had ridden in yesterday on the oddly marked paint mule. He himself had seen the man, heading up the canyon not two hours before the shooting must have taken place. Excitement rose within him.

"What did McGuire look like, Earl?" he asked, fighting to keep his voice and his expression calm.

Still frowning heavily, the marshal said, "Tall, dark, always wore a clean, gray Stetson, better than average clothes for a cowhand, rode good horses . . . hell, I don't remember. It's been a long time. He looked like a lot of folks, I reckon."

"Was he clean-shaven, or did he wear a beard?"

"Mustache, well-trimmed. Sort of a dandy, he was. Didn't like work much, either, as I remember. Why'n hell you asking, goddamnit? You know something or don't you?"

Cal stood up dejectedly. The description helped him little, if at all. It could have been his man—assuming a lot of changes—and assuming, even more, that the fellow wasn't dead after all!

"I guess not," he said. "I just happened to see a stranger yesterday, a man on a mule, heading upcanyon a while before dark. . . ."

"Well, it damn sure wasn't McGuire," Youngblood insisted. "Unless it was a dead man riding that mule, and I sorta doubt that's the case, don't you?"

"I suppose so," Cal admitted. "But I think I'll ask around about that mule rider. See if anyone else saw him." He could almost kick himself for not having followed that up last night, although he knew there was no way he could have known then that there was a need to. Even now, of course, he had no proof that the stranger had anything to do with the murders. But it was a possibility . . . and that was better than he could say for anything else he had learned so far.

Youngblood was looking at him curiously. "Well," he said after a few moments, "I hope something turns up for you. I do that."

"Yeah," Cal said, moving toward the door. "Don't we both."

2

From Doc Wagner's house, Cal went directly to the post office located inside Usery's General Store. He borrowed paper and pencil and wrote a short note to Tom Rudabaugh, then put it in the mail addressed to: Sheriff of Socorro County, Socorro, New Mexico Territory. From the post office, he proceeded past the jail to the mortuary, where he learned from Bay Calhoun that based on the personal effects found on the bodies of the La Belle brothers, robbery could almost certainly be ruled out as a motive for the killings. Pocket watches, knives, money—all there about as one would expect, all items that could easily have been taken had the killer so desired.

"Someone just plain laid down on 'em, Cal," the thin, dark son of an early Irish immigrant father and a Mexican mother said glumly. "And he didn't mind us knowing it, either. I'd say it's about as bad a looking deal as I've seen around here in a long time. I sure would."

"How do you mean?"

"A killing's a killing," Calhoun explained soberly, "and

they're all bad enough. But a cold-blooded murder from ambush like this . . . well, it makes you wonder. What if he
does it again? What if it's not just the La Belles he's got it in
for? Have you thought of that, Cal?"

Cal hadn't, and as he walked the short distance back up
the street to the jail where he had tied his horse, he somehow wished Bay Calhoun hadn't, either. It added to his
troubles a sense of possible urgency that the killer be found,
but in no way served to bring him closer to that end.

Inside the marshal's office he found Enos Cooper balanced
precariously with his crutch under one armpit, sweeping out
the jail cells. Quite obviously Enos had already heard about
the killings.

"You're just lucky you ain't got no customers inside here
to worry about just now," the jailer told him grumpily. "Unless, o' course, you got some idea who the murderin' sonofagun is that shot them two brothers down. Be good if you
had him in here, by damn!"

"That's the trouble, Enos. I've got no idea at all. Nobody
has."

Enos put aside his broom and hobbled into the office. He
took a chair beside the desk. "Yeah. I heard. Jeremy Chance
was just by . . . told me what you'd told him already." He
wagged his head. "It's a bad deal, boy. A damn bad deal."

"Everybody seems to agree on that," Cal said dourly.
"Can you think of anything that would help me, Enos?"

The older man shook his head. "I wish I could, son. But I
don't know nobody who'd do a thing like this. I just don't. I
know a lotta men who could kill another man, some without
battin' an eyelash. But shootin' from ambush like that . . . I
just don't know."

"Do you remember the stranger I asked you about yesterday?" Cal asked then. "The one riding a paint mule?"

"I remember you askin'."

"Have you seen or heard about anybody else who saw
him?"

Enos looked slightly exasperated. "No, can't say as I have. But I ain't been askin', either. Why? You got some sorta fixation on that stranger, boy?"

Cal shrugged. "I don't know. Maybe I do. But I did see him headed up the canyon not long before we figure the La Belles were shot last night. I'd like to at least find out who he is and where he was going."

Enos nodded thoughtfully. "Yeah, I guess you would. Which is only right. It's somethin' that oughta be checked out. You ask around yourself any, like I told you?"

"No," Cal admitted with a slight flinch, "but I aim to—if I can ever get in a word edgewise for people wanting to know about the killings. . . ." He paused. "You know, that's beginning to worry me some, too, Enos. I'm afraid the more people hear about this, the more some of them are going to start looking over their shoulders and wondering if it's going to happen again."

Enos gave him a long look, then nodded slowly. "That could be a problem, all right. 'Specially if everybody goes to carryin' guns and jumpin' at shadows ever' place they go. Don't know how you're gonna stop it, though; people are bound to learn about it and to want to know more once they do."

Cal shook his head. This thing just kept getting more and more complicated, his problems bigger and more profuse. "Well, I guess I can avoid going out of my way to hurry it along. The more time it takes for the story to get around the better, I guess."

Enos frowned. "I wouldn't put too much faith in that bein' very long, if I was you," he said. "Somethin' I was supposed to tell you. Caleb Harvey's already been lookin' for you. Had me promise to have you stop by his office. Wants to get all the dope he can before he puts it in the *Myriad* tomorrow. No way people ain't gonna find out and find out quick, once that happens."

Cal, faced with the inevitability of this, went out the door a few minutes later, convinced that nothing—absolutely nothing—was ever going to go right again.

3

The snow on the streets was becoming slushy by the time he delivered his horse to the livery stable and then trudged back up the street to the newspaper office. Actually, he could have delayed the trip, for the *Myriad* was located directly across from the jail. But he was putting that off, wishing as he did the first chore and then walked back up the street that it would all just get up and go away, yet knowing all the while that there was no way it would.

Something he was putting off even more than talking to Caleb was the chance of seeing Jenny face-to-face for the first time since that Saturday night he had taken her to the dance at the school. He realized this fully as he reached the front door and caught a glimpse of her through the window. She was standing toward the back of the office at the type cases, and he suddenly experienced an acute awkwardness at having to face her, even indirectly.

But any urge to turn away was immediately stifled; Caleb, sitting at his desk toward the front of the office, had already seen him and was coming to meet him at the door. Cal squared his shoulders and opened it.

"Hello, Caleb," he said, stepping inside. "Enos said you wanted to see me."

"Glad you could come by, Cal." Harvey put out a hand. Slight and wiry, the newspaperman nevertheless had a big man's way of looking at a person, a sharp, sure gaze coming out of deep brown eyes set beneath heavy black brows, a slightly slanted forehead and receding hairline, and with an intense set of the jaw that could distract even a studied gaze from the lines of age etched in his clean-shaven face. He wore dark gray pants, a black vest, and an ink-stained blue-striped shirt. "We haven't seen a lot of you lately, Cal," he added meaningfully.

Cal could see Jenny out the corner of his eye and was keenly aware that she had at first been watching him but was now looking away and had made no move to come forward or say anything. He returned Caleb's straightforward look but refrained trying to explain away his absence of late. The truth, he knew, hardly needed to be stated. "I guess you want to know about the killings."

"Anything and everything, boy," the other man said. "All you know." He went over to retake his own seat behind the desk.

Cal knew there was no use arguing that the story be held back; he had known it when he left the marshal's office a while earlier. Caleb Harvey was a good newspaperman, and news of the La Belle killings would be in the next issue of his paper even if he had to stay up all night to get it in. Of a good newspaperman, nothing less could be asked.

Cal took a chair across the desk from Caleb. "Where do you want me to start?"

Caleb reached into a desk drawer and drew out paper and pencil, then said, "From the first . . . who found them, what time, and exactly where? In the cabin? Outside the cabin? Had they been dead long . . . you know—an hour, six hours, a day? Every detail you can think of, Cal, that's what I want."

Cal related the incident as precisely and accurately as he knew how, stopping only when the other man interrupted to ask a question or to clarify a point. At no time did the newspaperman seem to get behind in the recording of key details, and by the time Cal had finished, he had a page and a half of notes written in legible longhand.

"Well!" he said, shaking his head. "I can't complain about not having any news to print this week, can I?"

Cal gave him a not-too-happy smile but said nothing.

"Do you know what you're going to do about it?" Caleb

asked. "Have you any idea how to go about finding the killer?"

"Well, I've already written Tom Rudabaugh about it, for one thing. He's sheriff of this county and about the only other lawman around who has jurisdiction. Fact is—now that I think about it—he may be the only one who fits that criterion. It happened outside Grafton proper, you know."

Harvey gave him a studied look. "You know how it is for the mining towns up here. The only real law we have is what we hire ourselves, in *and* outside of town. You'll be lucky if Tom Rudabaugh even answers your letter."

Cal smiled thinly. "I've got to try, Caleb. We need help, and I've got no credentials as a lawman. You know that."

Caleb Harvey had a very sincere look on his face then. "I have a feeling you'll measure up, though," he said. "You're conscientious, and your kind does when it has to. I've observed that many times." It was a simple but profound compliment, coming from a man who was given neither to triviality nor cheap praise. Cal could only wish he shared the confidence and doubly so that he might be deserving of it.

After a moment he said, "I don't suppose you have any ideas, Caleb—about who might have wanted the La Belle boys dead."

Harvey rubbed his chin thoughtfully. "Well, if, as you say, robbery is out as a motive, and neither of them had any mining claims of their own staked out somewhere—which I'm sure they didn't, or they wouldn't have been working at the Glory Be . . ." He shook his head. "I'm afraid I just don't know, Cal. I've just never heard of anything the La Belles ever mixed in that would have made them an enemy like this. Of course, that doesn't mean there couldn't have been something." He paused suddenly, evidently reading something in Cal's expression. "You've got something on your mind, haven't you? What is it?"

"What do you know about a man named Guthrie McGuire? Did you know him?"

Caleb's eyebrows raised. "I should say I did! Caused something of a stir around here once. But why? He's dead now. Surely if you've heard of him, you've heard that."

Cal nodded. "I've heard. But I want to be sure. I was told there was a newspaper story about his death. Have you seen it?"

"Matter of fact, I have," Caleb said. "Came out in the Santa Fe *Republican*. Someone sent me a copy of the issue, and someone else fetched one back from Santa Fe about the same time. Most everybody heard about it. Happened not long after he broke jail."

"Do you still have your copy?"

"I think so. But it's probably in the back room. You want to wait while I go have a look?"

"If you don't mind."

Caleb rose and came around the desk. He was just going through the swinging gate in the rail that separated the front office from the much larger working area in the rear when he stopped and turned back.

"Maybe you'd like to visit with Jenny while I'm gone," he suggested, just loud enough that the girl couldn't help but hear. Then, in a lowered voice, "I meant it when I said we've missed you lately, boy. At least Martha and I have. And I think the girl has too—despite what else you may have heard." He left this last hanging in the air with a meaningful glance, then disappeared through a door in the back, leaving Jenny and Cal suddenly staring awkwardly at one another across fifty feet of room.

The girl turned slightly, picked up a cloth beside the job case where she had been setting type, and wiped her hands. She was a tall girl with a slim waist and firm, high breasts that were not large at all for a big girl but still stood out revealingly against her ink-stained apron and shirtwaist underneath. That she had a pretty face was indisputable, although most would not have thought her beautiful. She had high cheekbones, clear white skin that held just the right hint of color, depthless hazel eyes that could cut as well as sparkle, and long blond hair that could be brushed to a golden sheen whenever she so desired but that now looked slightly disheveled. A few strands held together lightly by perspiration lay against her forehead and down over one check, and an ink smudge showed on one side of her nose.

She came forward, stopping only when she reached the rail. "I heard what Uncle said. I hope you weren't embarrassed on my account."

"Should I have been?" he asked a little stiffly.

She shook her head more in uncertainty than in denial. "Only if you've avoided coming around for the reason everyone thinks you have. You know what that is, don't you?"

Cal could only manage a puzzled frown, and wasn't at all sure what to say. Finally he looked around, spotted the chair he had been sitting in only moments before, and went over to drag it across the floor. "Don't you want to sit down? Looks to me like you'd get tired standing in front of those type cases all day."

She smiled then. "Yes, you're right. I do get tired. Uncle broke the stool that goes there a week ago and hasn't gotten another one made." She came through the swinging gate and took the chair. Cal relaxed against the rail but did not sit down.

"You didn't answer my question," she said shortly. "It's because of Quentin Usery, isn't it? You don't approve of my seeing him, do you?"

"I doubt if it's up to me to approve who you do or don't see," Cal said. "Not even any of my business, probably."

An instant trace of surprise and possibly hurt crossed her face, as if this was anything but what she had hoped he would say. She seemed almost like a child exhibiting a need for discipline, wanting him to be at least a little bit jealous or possessive. For a moment, it made Cal feel good that she might react this way—but then he asked himself: If she wants me, why is she messing around with Usery?—and the good feeling suddenly vanished.

"How serious is it between you and Quentin?" he asked abruptly.

There was an immediate flash of hazel as she said, "I suppose that *is* some of your business . . . or did I simply ask the wrong question before?"

Cal stared at her for a moment before saying, "No, you didn't ask the wrong question. I'm sorry. I was wrong."

Jenny accepted the apology coolly. "There's not that much between Quentin and me," she said. "He simply has been attentive and interested, and he's asked to escort me to church and a dance"—she paused meaningfully—"and he's been around when you haven't, Cal. Maybe I just figured you didn't care to come back."

Again, Cal stared at her. He hadn't thought of it from this viewpoint before at all. He had been busy at the ranch for the couple of weeks following the dance he had taken her to, then he had heard about her and Quentin, and finally, he supposed, he had felt hurt and rejected. Now he wasn't sure what to think.

"Are you saying that just because I didn't come around for a couple of weeks you took up with Usery?"

"I did not 'take up' with anybody," she said indignantly. "I'm just saying he has shown his interest by being attentive. You have not."

"I guess I just don't have the time on my hands that he does," Cal said bitterly. "Maybe if I had all the money I need and hired help running out my ears—"

Jenny was shaking her head vigorously. "He *makes* time, Cal. Maybe because he's just a bit more interested. . . ."

Cal rose to this challenge even before she finished making it. "Okay," he said, "let's just see about that. Is there a dance at the school Saturday night? Will you go with me if there is?"

Her face fell instantly. "Oh Cal—I can't! I mean . . . there is a dance, but Quentin has already asked me."

Cal looked straight up at the ceiling and was about to say something when he sensed, then turned to see, Caleb Harvey standing not ten feet away. He had walked up very quietly, and it was impossible to tell if he had heard any of what had been said.

If he had, he didn't let on, for he came forward without saying a word about it. In his hand was a two-month-old copy of the Santa Fe *Republican*.

"Don't know why I had so much trouble remembering where I put this," he said, handing it to Cal. "Hasn't been that long since I filed it. Here it is, anyway. Right there on the second page."

As Jenny excused herself and headed back toward the job case, Cal began reading the story Caleb had pointed out. It was short and simple beneath a bold-face headline that proclaimed:

ESCAPED PRISONER FOUND DEAD NEAR LAS VEGAS

The body of a man believed to be Guthrie McGuire was found recently on Sapello Creek in the mountains north and west of Las Vegas. The dead man was the apparent victim of a brutal mauling by a bear and may be remembered by Santa Feans as the prisoner who escaped the penitentiary recently after stabbing one guard to death and seriously wounding another.

Although facial features were destroyed beyond recognition by the mauling, identification was made from articles of clothing and personal effects found on the body—all of which are now known to have belonged to McGuire. Further confirmation comes from the fact that a man calling himself McGuire (and wearing the same clothing as found on the victim) was reported seen outside Las Vegas only a few days before by two cowhands of the Jess Traylor ranch. Both cowhands later stated that the man openly boasted who he was and of his recent escape from the Santa Fe prison.

McGuire, convicted of cattle stealing in Socorro County, had served better than two years of his prison sentence prior to his escape.

Twice Cal read the article and both times his eyes traveled back to the words "facial features were destroyed beyond recognition . . ." He looked at Caleb. "Do you accept this? It leaves no question in your mind that McGuire is dead?"

Caleb's gaze was a penetrating one. "Why shouldn't I accept it? Prison clothing and personal effects that were known to be McGuire's. The man having been seen only a few days before, boasting who he was. Why shouldn't I?"

Cal thought for a long moment, then sighed. "I guess you're right. It does look pretty conclusive."

"What makes you so interested in McGuire, anyway?" Caleb asked, a look of intrigue on his face. "Who told you about him?"

"Clayt Usery mentioned him to me," Cal said. "And I'm not sure why I'm so interested. He's someone who might have reason to hold a grudge against people in this town—at least it looks that way to me. Someone who might shoot two men down in cold blood . . ."

The look in Caleb's eyes was very much like that in Earl Youngblood's when that individual had been quizzed about McGuire earlier. "Don't you think that's a little farfetched, Cal—when you already know the man is dead?"

Cal shrugged. "I don't know. Maybe it is, maybe it isn't."

"What else did Usery tell you? Did he say anything about McGuire's wife?"

"Not much," Cal said. Then: "Why? You know, I'm getting some mighty curious reactions to my questions about McGuire. Makes me wonder if his influence—and maybe his wife's too—wasn't more than it seems it should have been to this town."

Caleb shrugged this time. "Could be . . . but it doesn't matter now. They're both dead, and I see no way they could have anything to do with what's happened today. I'd advise another tack, my boy, I surely would."

Cal handed the paper back to Caleb. "Maybe you're right," he said in an unconvinced tone. "Anyhow, thanks for letting me see this. And if you think of anything else, let me know." He cast a glance toward the back of the office, but did not catch Jenny's eye.

"One more thing," he said before turning toward the door to leave. "You didn't happen to see a stranger on a paint mule ride through here late yesterday, did you?"

Caleb gave him a blank look. "No, I don't believe I did. Why?"

Cal shook his head, beginning to wonder now if he himself hadn't been seeing things. "Just thought I'd ask," he said.

4

Less than fifteen miles away Guthrie McGuire had found an abandoned prospector's cabin nestled well within the rising slopes of the Black Range. He had known about it already, had known that it had been abandoned three years before, and had gone looking for it in hopes that it still was.

Just finding it had been hard enough; for over two hours he had ridden around lost in the snowstorm. And then, when he had found it, he had been momentarily uncertain that it was still abandoned. But it had been pitch dark on the inside, no smoke coming from the chimney, the door standing half ajar, and there were no animals to be seen in the corral out back . . . sign enough that the place was indeed unoccupied.

Inside he found it almost as cold as it was on the outside, but it was protection from the wind, and once the door was pushed shut and a small fire was started in the fireplace, things quickly warmed up. It had made do for the night, which was all he could really ask of it at the time.

Next morning, however, he quickly set about making things more livable. The floor was dirt, and in places was muddy from the snow that had blown in through the half-open door and then had quickly melted from the warmth coming from the fireplace. These places simply had to be avoided until dry. But other shortcomings could be remedied: cobwebs and dust swept away, rats' nests burned, holes in the floor filled in, the few now-useless pieces of furniture that had not already been removed broken up for firewood, and even a bed, built of pine boughs, fashioned in a spot out away from spider-infested walls and corners.

By noon he was satisfied if not completely happy. He had shelter—located well off any beaten path and probably forgotten by most—and for now, that was all he needed. In the canyon bottom nearby was a small spring with drinkable water, he carried food for at least a week in his gear—salt, flour, and coffee for even longer—and there had always been plenty of wild game for the taking in the hills around.

By midafternoon the snow was melting some and he had even found a bluff-sheltered spot where the grass was tall enough that he could stake the mule out to graze. Later he led her to the spring to drink, then put her back in the corral. Just before dark, he shot a couple of cottontails and cooked them on a spit over the fire in the fireplace. He ate them both with relish; then, with only the fire for light, he sat cross-legged on the floor and pulled a scrap of paper from his shirt pocket. On the paper was a list of names, scrawled months ago in the dim light of his prison cell. They were in no particular order, but already crossed off were those of Jess and Hiram La Belle. Catching his eye next was that of Little Mike Wonderly, the town's butcher.

Idly, he wondered if Little Mike still lived in the same house in town near the Victorio Mine road. It didn't really matter much, he figured, except that it might make things a bit easier if he did.

Before, it had been the last house on that edge of town.

FOUR

DIVERSIONS

1

Jeremy Chance stopped by the marshal's office, a somewhat vague look on his face and apparently with an even more vague purpose in mind.

"Heard there was a fight over at the Pioneer last night," he said, coming across to stand in front of the stove. He removed his gloves and rubbed his hands together vigorously; the sky had remained clear overnight, and the early-morning air was like ice outside. "You know about it?"

Cal looked up from his desk and nodded. "I knew. I broke it up."

"Oh?" Jeremy evidently had not heard that part of the story.

"And it wasn't the Pioneer, it was the California. Two miners fighting over Abronia Garcia, one of the girls who works for Gutierrez."

Chance wagged his head. "Well, I'll be damned! Guess that shows how mixed up a second-hand story can get. Did you have any trouble breaking it up?" The blacksmith was a member of the town committee and apparently knew of Cal's concern over being able to keep the peace.

"Not much," Cal said casually, thinking how ironic it was that breaking up fights at the saloon had once seemed his biggest problem. Once. "I've got them both cooling off in the back room right now. Figured I'd let them out this morning, soon as they're good and sobered up."

Jeremy frowned. "Hadn't heard that, either. Maybe that's why Quentin Usery's in town so early. . . . Either of those two men work at one of the Usery mines, Cal?"

"Probably both of them," Cal said. "And I see what you're getting at . . . only I thought I made it clear to Clayt that I wouldn't tolerate any troublemakers, *regardless* of who they work for."

"Making something clear to Clayt," Jeremy warned in a meaningful tone, "is not necessarily the same as making it clear to Quentin. Things aren't right between those two, Cal. Thought you knew that."

Cal shrugged. "I suppose I did. But I also thought Clayt was boss when it came to the Usery enterprises. I didn't know you had to deal with them both on everything."

"I don't know that you do," Jeremy said. "But things have changed in the past year or so. May not be all that noticeable to some, but changed just the same. Quentin's become more independent, and Clayt . . . well, I don't know. He's weakened, it seems to me, begun losing control. I'm not sure why, but he's not the same man he was. Still boss maybe, but only so long as he doesn't push it too hard. Maybe it's the trouble he and Cora are having, maybe it's something else . . . I don't know. But it is something, I can tell you that."

Cal thought about this and found it an interesting observation, maybe even a disturbing one. He tended to agree with Caleb Harvey: The Userys ran Grafton, and had for some time; in many ways they *were* Grafton. And instinctively, if this were going to be the case, Cal would much rather have Clayt in charge than Quentin. The former was generally benevolent, at least where his own interets were not threatened; the latter was anything but.

"Well," Jeremy said, pulling his gloves back on, "I've got six horses over at my place that'll never get shod if I don't get a move on. Don't suppose you'd like to come by and lend a hand after a bit?"

Cal gave him a thoughtful look. "I might just do that," he said seriously. "Soon as Enos gets back."

Jeremy looked around, as if only now becoming aware that there was a missing fixture about the place. "Where is that old reprobate, anyway?"

"Over at the hotel having breakfast," Cal told him with a smile. "He was going to the doc's house to visit Earl after that. I told him I thought I could hold down the fort till he got back."

Jeremy laughed. "Sometimes I think that old sonofagun actually believes he's the marshal around here."

"Lately," Cal said, "I've been wishing he was!"

Jeremy laughed again as he reached for the door. "Give it a chance, Cal. You might even learn to like it."

Fat chance! Cal thought as he watched the door close behind the blacksmith. *Fat chance I might!*

2

Half an hour later Enos showed up and Cal brought out the two miners he had jailed the night before. Neither man appeared particularly chastised, but their belligerence had evaporated somewhere inside their separate cells during the night, along with their drunkenness. Each seemed glad enough to be getting out of jail as soon as he was.

Enos watched as Cal gave them back their belongings and released them. "I'd a-kept 'em in there a week if it'd a-been me," the jailer spat after they were gone.

"I just wanted them to sleep it off," Cal explained patiently. "No call to keep them any longer. They didn't do anything that bad."

"Humph!" Enos grunted. But that was all he said. He

looked around sharply as Cal pulled on his sheepskin and donned his hat. "Where you goin'?"

"I told Jeremy Chance I'd drop by and help him shoe some horses." Then with a little glint in his eye: "Reckon you can handle things around here for a while?"

Enos shot him a look. "I been a-doin' it, ain't I?"

Outside, Cal stood on the boardwalk for a few moments, breathing deeply of the cold, clear air and studying the street. Already the day was beginning to warm and soon the frozen ruts in the mud before him would be thawing, becoming a quagmire by afternoon. And the snow on the hillsides beyond town, although melting little yesterday, would begin to go fast today. Small rivulets of water would run briefly down the canyon bottoms and into the arroyo that ran through town; and by day after tomorrow—save another storm, of course—snow would exist only in patches on the north-facing slopes of hills, in shaded canyon bottoms, in deeper drifts, and on the higher mountain slopes to the west.

That was the way with early storms in this part of the country; they came and went rapidly, as did their aftermath. Cal was glad for it too, for already his few head of cattle would be pawing through snow for grass to eat and by tomorrow would be grazing normally on open grassy flats and hillsides. He might ride out this afternoon sometime to check on those he could find, but otherwise no special care would have to be taken because of the storm.

His eyes drifted back to the street. At the far end of town he could just see a Southwestern Stage Company Concorde sitting in front of the stage office, a fresh team stamping and pulling against their harness. He thought of his letter to Tom Rudabaugh in Socorro, thinking that by tomorrow, at least, he should have news of the killings in hand. He wondered if it would do any good, and told himself once again not to count on it.

He was just about to turn in the direction of the livery stable when he noticed Quentin Usery come out of the Manor House and mount a bay horse that had been tied to the hitch rail there. He waited as he saw Usery rein the horse in his direction. A few seconds later the man pulled up alongside the boardwalk where Cal stood but did not dismount.

The tone of his voice was less than friendly. "I was aiming to look you up this morning, Sawyer. I see you've already let my two men loose."

Cal eyed him imperturbably. "Yes, I let them go."

"Too late for them to make the shift wagon for the mines, too, I notice." Usery's words were stiff but his face remained impassive, as if it really didn't matter that much about the two miners—as if it were no more than a convenient point on which he might establish that he had no intention of being cordial.

Sensing this, Cal reacted with a moment's silent study. Quentin Usery had both the style and face of a gambler: lean, square-jawed, slightly dark, his mustache black and sleek and his eyes keen yet almost impossible to fully engage. He was about Cal's height, medium of build, and always wore good clothes. Like with a gambler, one could almost never tell what was on his mind.

"It didn't occur to me about the shift wagons," Cal finally said. "I let them out as soon as I thought they were ready to get out. They probably wouldn't have been much good to you anyway, today."

It was more obvious than ever now that this was not the subject Usery meant to pursue. He waved an impatient hand in the air. "Yeah, well, I'll let it go at that. But only because what I really want to know is what are you going to do about the La Belle killings?"

Cal's eyes narrowed. "I'm not sure I follow you," he said slowly. "What is it you expect me to do?"

"Why, find the killer, of course," Usery said. "What else?"

Cal almost laughed. "I thought maybe you had something specific in mind. Like, maybe, how to go about that little chore."

Usery's face darkened noticeably. "*That* is what we hired you to know."

"'We'? Who do you mean 'we'?" It was not the question that bothered Cal; it was the way it was asked. "I was hired by the town committee—your brother, Jeremy Chance, and Bay Calhoun. I wasn't aware you were on the committee too."

"I'm not," Usery said coldly. "But I am a citizen of this town and I have men out at the mines who are pretty worked up about this deal. Some of them are even scared because they think it might happen to them next. And I figure I have a right to ask what you're doing about it."

Cal relaxed slightly. Usery was right about this and they both knew it. "I'm doing what I can," he said. "I never promised any more than that." Then, to the other man's look of impatient dissatisfaction, he went on to explain. "There's not really a lot I can do. I've sent word to Tom Rudabaugh in Socorro, I've checked out every lead I've had—which has been virtually none—and I'll continue to check anywhere or anytime I have a chance to learn something. Beyond that, I guess all I can say is that I'm open to suggestions. I'm sorry, but that's about it."

"You have absolutely no idea who did the shooting? Not even a suspect?"

Cal eyed him coolly for several seconds, then said, "What do you remember about a man named Guthrie McGuire? He was sent to prison for cattle rustling around here a few years ago, I understand."

Usery looked surprised. "I remember him for just that—an ordinary cowthief sent to prison for what he did. Why? What's he got to do with anything?"

"Well, from what I hear he's a man who might hold a

grudge for what happened to him. A man whose wife died right here, only a year ago—"

"The man's dead, Sawyer," Usery snapped coldly. "And who told you about him? About the woman, his wife?"

"Why, your brother, as a matter of fact."

Usery stared as if from disbelief, then wagged his head. "What else did he tell you . . . exactly?"

"Not much," Cal said, remembering how someone else— he thought Earl Youngblood—had reacted with almost the precise same question. "He was caught and convicted of stealing cattle, sent to prison, later broke out, and was supposedly killed a couple of months ago up near Las Vegas. About the wife, Clayt told me almost nothing."

Once more Usery shook his head. "It's a damn wonder that," he muttered as if to himself. Then quickly: "In any event, he did tell you that McGuire is dead. That means he couldn't have had anything to do with the killings—"

"He was *reported* dead," Cal clarified. "There's a possible difference that only I seem unwilling to rule out—but a difference just the same. . . ." He let his words trail off as he realized that Quentin Usery was of a sudden hardly listening. There was a faraway look in his eyes, as if an intriguing thought of significant proportions had just struck him.

"What is it? What are you thinking?"

The other man seemed startled. "Huh? Oh . . . nothing. Nothing. I was just thinking, that's all."

"Well, anyway," Cal went on, "there's one more thing. Day before yesterday, just before the snow hit, I met a stranger riding through town on a spotted mule. I haven't been able to find anyone else who saw him then or since but . . ." He looked Usery in the eye. "I don't suppose you were in town and happened to see this fellow? It was before the shift wagons came in, maybe as much as an hour."

Usery hesitated for a long moment, and at first Cal actually thought the man was going to say "Yes." But instead his shook his head. "No . . . no, I didn't see anyone like that. I must have left town before he rode through. . . ." His words trailed away as his mind seemed to churn strangely behind the gambler's mask he wore for a face.

All of a sudden he straightened in the saddle. "I've got to be going, Sawyer. Have to get out to the mines. Just remember, though: I've got a lot of men out there who are damned anxious about this deal. Don't forget that."

"Don't worry," Cal said, still a little mystified by the man's reaction to his questions about the stranger on the spotted mule. "I won't."

Usery started to rein away then, but turned back as if from an afterthought. "Another thing," he said. "I guess you know I've been seeing Miss Bayles."

"Yes, I know," Cal said warily.

"And that I'll be taking her to the dance Saturday night?"

"I'd heard that. Why?"

He gave Cal a long, pointed look. "Just so you know," he said, and without another word turned and rode away.

3

Cal helped Jeremy Chance shoe horses till noon, then saddled his grulla and rode out to the homestead. There was not a lot he had to do there; most of his belongings were secure inside the small cabin he had built himself last spring, and most of the rest were kept inside one of two lean-to sheds out back. He had no chickens or milch cow to tend to (he planned to acquire both as soon as he had the money, which, with his pay as temporary town marshal, might now come even sooner than originally expected); and the dozen or so range cattle he was able to locate grazing on nearby south-facing slopes where the snow was melting fastest seemed to be faring well enough for themselves. The others, about fifty cows and three bulls, he figured, were somewhere around and doing about the same.

Presently he sat the grulla looking thoughtfully down on the cabin and sheds from a nearby hillside. He had searched long and hard before deciding on the spot: the bottom of a pretty canyon where tall pines rose in stately calm above a grassy bench that was tailor-made for the homesite and twenty-acre field of dryland corn that had been his pride and joy all summer long. A small stream ran intermittently in the canyon bottom; a dug well about a hundred feet from the cabin provided water for the house; and in good years grama grass hay could be cut from the bench beyond the cornfield. All summer Cal had worked to build a fence around the field, and next summer, to supplement the well and make irrigation water available for a garden, he planned to build a cistern and ditch water to it from the creek whenever the latter ran clear in the spring and fall.

It wasn't easy to make a go of it as a homesteader, and certainly there was no promise of becoming rich for having done so. A good job at the mines would have paid him much better, at least for now. But he was convinced, too, that the mines wouldn't last; the future of this country was cattle . . . the vast, renewable resource of good grass, the reasonably mild climate ridded now of the Apache menace and awaiting only those visionary few who were already filtering in to make their start. Clayton Usery had seen this, and so had Lige Martin and Frank Simpson, Cal's nearest neighbors a few miles to the south. They, too, had ranches, growing cattle herds, a shipping point now only fifty miles away at Magdalena. It was they and a few others like them who had already begun to change the character of Grafton from that of a mining camp to a real town, maybe even that of a full-fledged ranching community someday. They were a settling influence that brought signs of normalcy and permanency and a true sense of the future. Men with families who were as concerned about building schools and churches as they were with more saloons. Decent women and their children, girls and young women—although admittedly still few in number—whom a man could take to a dance now and then. . . .

Which was a sign in itself—the Saturday night dances at the schoolhouse. These had begun since Cal's own arrival in Grafton, in the last year, and were very definitely not a custom spawned by the mining camp atmosphere. They weren't even generally attended by the miners; they were affairs suited mostly to the scattered ranch families, local townsmen, cowhands looking to socialize with decent girls. Cal supposed this reflected a division already evident between the two segments of the fledgling society, and that it was a natural one that would probably exist—and maybe even grow as time went on—as long as both segments managed to persist in the same community. The miners were simply a different breed, and about the only thing that would change the situation would be when and if the mines closed down for good. The miners would either leave or become something else and fit themselves into the community in an entirely different way. And that might not be a bad thing, either. Especially from a town marshal's point of view. . . .

Cal shook himself, not liking this train of thought at all. He had no intention of acquiring a lawman's point of view, certainly not in so long range a way as that! His thoughts turned back to the dances, to the coming Saturday night and Jenny. He couldn't help seething every time he thought of the way Quentin Usery had so boldly warned him away from her earlier in the day. He wondered, did the man really think he could eliminate his competition so easily as that? In a way it was almost a good sign that he thought he needed to; it certainly did not spell self-confidence. No way that!

Suddenly he realized how lost in thought he had become. He lifted his gaze to the west. The sun, which had beamed down reasonably warm through the middle of the day, had lowered considerably now, and the Black Range was already casting cold shadows his way. Sundown would come in less than an hour, and Cal was forced to admit that he wasn't going to solve any of his problems sitting where he was. Especially those having to do with Jenny Bayles.

He rode back to town, had supper at the Chinaman's for a change, and checked in at the jail. After that he made the rounds checking door locks on stores up and down Main Street and then the saloons. Things seemed quiet, almost subdued from the Blake to the Pioneer, and by nine o'clock Cal realized he was tired and maybe just a little down in the mouth. When he headed for his room at the hotel a short while later, a good night's sleep was about the only thing on his mind.

4

A voice called to him just as he reached the head of the stairs at the hotel. A slender, dark-haired figure stood before an open doorway less than thirty feet away. It was Cora Usery.

"Cal. Please. Can I talk to you?"

She made no move to leave the doorway, however, so Cal walked on over to where she stood. "What is it? Is there something wrong?"

She looked both ways, then back at Cal. "I hope you won't think me brazen . . . but will you come inside? Please."

He didn't know whether the beseeching look on her face was a measure of how badly she wanted him to enter the room or her concern that he not think her brazen. He hadn't even known she had a room on the second floor . . . at least, he assumed it was her room. If it was, she didn't appear to have been there long, or at least had not been preparing for bed; she was fully clothed, even to the point of still wearing the long, frilly apron she used to wait tables downstairs.

"Of course," he told her. "I don't mind, if you don't."

Her expression was thankful as she led him inside and closed the door. He looked around and quickly concluded that it was indeed a woman's room: It was clean, neat, the air notably absent of tobacco smoke, and with feminine articles such as hair brushes and ribbons in full display on the dressing table; and on the bed, a couple of chemises. . . . Cal's eyes settled on these for just an instant and were then jerked away in such obvious embarrassment that Cora laughed. She went over and picked up the undergarments and put them inside a drawer, then motioned toward a chair across the room from the bed.

"Please sit down, Cal."

He took the chair as directed and asked, "What is it? What did you want to talk to me about?"

She settled herself on the foot of the bed, her hands clasped in her lap and her shoulder against the brass bedstead. "It's Clayt and Quentin, Cal. They argued tonight, right here in the hotel. I—I overheard them . . . in the room Quentin sometimes uses to stay in town overnight downstairs. It was a terrible argument."

Slightly perplexed, Cal said, "Brothers do argue sometimes, Cora. I mean . . ."

She shook her head vigorously. "Not at their age. Not like this. Oh it was terrible, Cal! I thought they were actually going to fight!"

"Do you know what they were arguing about?"

"Not for sure. Only that they were yelling and cursing and that Quentin came storming out and slammed out of the hotel looking like a thundercloud about to burst. And . . . I did hear your name mentioned once, Cal. Yours and the La Belles' and, I couldn't be sure, but I think that of a man named McGuire. Do you know anything about him, Cal?"

"A little," he said, suddenly alert. "Do you?"

"Only the name. I've heard it mentioned a couple of times, along with that of his wife . . . what was her name? Cathy?"

"Cassie," Cal corrected.

"Oh yes. Well, anyway, I overheard something once that caused me to ask Clayt about her—I can't remember what it was now—but he wouldn't say much. Nobody seems to want to say much about either of them. Sort of hush-hush, for some reason. The woman died very shortly before I came here, I think . . . and McGuire was sent to prison or something, sometime before that."

"Yet you think Clayt and Quentin were arguing about him tonight," Cal said, pondering. "Do you have any idea why? Didn't you hear anything said besides the name?"

"No, not really. And I didn't say they were arguing about him. I just said I thought I heard his name." But then something about Cal's expression must have caused her to wonder. "Why *would* they argue about McGuire, Cal? And why would your name and that of the La Belles come up at the same time?"

Cal shook his head. "That's what I'd like to know. McGuire, like his wife, is supposed to be dead. It's said he was mauled by a bear up near Las Vegas a couple of months ago. I read a newspaper account of it yesterday."

Cora obviously didn't understand. "Then why would his name come up now?"

"My fault, I guess. It was something Clayt said up at the La Belle cabin right after the murders were discovered. I've been asking questions about McGuire ever since. Oh I know, he's supposed to be dead. But these killings were revenge killings, I'd swear to that. And from what I can learn, McGuire is one man who might have held a grudge against some of the people in this town."

"But why? Who?"

"Well, I'm not sure if this is all there is to it, but he was sent to prison from here, and his wife died here after he was gone."

"And the La Belles? What did they have to do with any of that?"

Cal shrugged. "From what I've learned so far they were not only members of the posse that brought him in, but also testified against him at his trial. No question he'd remember that. Maybe . . ."

"But Cal, if he's dead . . ." There was an apologetic look of disbelief on her face.

"I know, I know," Cal said. "But listen. I'll admit the reports of his death were pretty positive. Yet the one I saw was also anything but conclusive. The dead man was mauled beyond recognition, it said; he was identified only by the clothing he wore and the fact that McGuire was supposed to have been seen in the area a few days before. I say it's possible—remotely, maybe—but just possible that Guthrie McGuire is not dead."

The doubtful look on her face remained sympathetic but did not fade. "Oh Cal . . . you're grabbing at straws, surely you are."

He started to tell her then about the stranger on the spotted mule, but even he had yet to put the two things together in any positive way, and thus decided it would only further confuse the issue. Nevertheless, he said stubbornly, "Okay, maybe I am, but tell me this: Why were Clayt and Quentin arguing about him tonight? Why that?"

"I don't know," she said, shaking her head very slowly. "I just know it was an awful argument. And it's not the first time. Cal, I think Quentin hates Clayt. I don't know for sure why. Quentin wants control of the mines, and Clayt won't give it to him, I know that. But it's more too . . . something I don't understand and Clayt won't tell me about." A pensive expression crossed her face then. "Not that he tells me about anything else either . . . anymore."

"Is that why you moved out on him?"

She looked up, a trace of hurt surprise in her eyes. "I didn't move out on him, Cal. It wasn't me, it was him. He wanted me to leave."

He instantly regretted not only the question but also the

way he had asked it. It had been totally unnecessary. "I'm sorry. I didn't know. I just sort of assumed. . . ."

"I know," she said, waving the apology off as unnecessary. "No one ever figures an old man can keep a young woman happy. Some people even think I married him because he is rich. But it's not true, none of it. I could be happy with Clayt, I really could. And I've tried very hard. But he is an unhappy man. Unhappy and haunted . . . I don't know by what, but very much haunted. It was *I* who couldn't make *him* happy. And so here I am, a wife but not a wife and not knowing what to do to make things better between us."

Cal shook his head. "A man would have to be nuts not to be happy with a woman like you, Cora."

She gave him an appreciative but wan smile. "There's a woman in Clayt Usery's life who he'll forever miss, but she's not me, Cal. She may never be me."

"His first wife," Cal said, drawing the obvious conclusion. "I don't know that I've ever heard her name, but . . ."

"Hannah," Cora said. "But somehow I don't think it's her, either. I've been married to Clayt for almost a year now, and I don't think I've heard him mention his first wife's name even twice.

"I hate to say it this way, Cal, but she's been dead for seven years, and my husband is not a man haunted by something seven years gone. Whoever or whatever it was, it's been much more recent than that."

Cal pondered this with something akin to amazement. "But you have no idea who or what."

She shook her head wistfully. "No . . . no, I don't. And I didn't ask you here to burden you with that part of my troubles, either. Forgive me, will you? The thing between Clayt and Quentin this evening frightened me so . . . well, I just had to have someone to confide in and I couldn't think of anyone but you. I hope you don't mind."

"No, I don't mind," he reassured, "but I'm not sure I can do much to help, either. Are you really afraid?"

"Yes—very. For Clayt mostly, I guess."

"Of what? That Quentin will actually do his own brother harm?"

"Quentin is a man without scruples, Cal. Maybe you don't believe that. . . ."

"I believe it," he said glumly, not entirely certain whence his conviction came, but somehow certain nevertheless. "Has Quentin ever done anything physically violent before? Has he threatened Clayt?"

She shook her head. "Not that I know of. Unless tonight . . . something I didn't hear."

"Well, I don't think we should assume that Clayt Usery is necessarily a man who can't take care of himself, but I am glad you told me what you did anyway. If the time ever comes that I can do anything, I'll know better how to act."

"And I will feel better that you know," Cora said gratefully.

There was a moment of silence then, after which Cal rose from his chair. "I suspect I should be going. My room is down the hall if you ever need anything. Number eleven."

She walked him to the door, where they stopped and looked at one another. Cora said, "It's not every day I invite a handsome man who's not my husband into my room, Cal. I want to thank you for not presuming anything."

He smiled. "Do you want to check the hall to make sure no one sees me leave?"

She cocked her head thoughtfully. "Maybe I should at that." She cracked the door open just enough that she could get her head through and look both ways. "All clear," she said, pulling back. "Good night, good friend."

He stepped quietly into the hall. "Good night, Cora."

He went to his room, his mind no longer even remotely on sleep.

FIVE

DEATH AGAIN

1

He almost didn't go to the dance Saturday night, but then he remembered that as marshal he was at least partially responsible for overseeing the goings-on there, and he was forced to change his mind.

Ordinarily, the affairs were pretty well policed by the participants themselves: Firearms were religiously checked at the schoolhouse door, while fist fights, liquor, and other such apparently necessary evils as drunken behavior and bad language were banished to the yard outside. But Cal knew (and Enos Cooper was quick to remind him of the fact) that Earl Youngblood had always made an appearance or two just to make sure everyone knew he was on hand. Thus Cal watched in not too appreciative a mood throughout the late-morning and afternoon hours as the ranch families and cowhands straggled into town, arriving aboard everything from buckboards and buggies to cowponies, and in no way demured either by the recent storm or, apparently, the news almost all had heard by now of the La Belle murders. As always, an air of happy celebration accompanied them, which was, in fact, the first real lightheartedness to be felt around Grafton since before the snow.

And Cal knew that not having a girl to take was no real reason to stay away from the excitement, either. As many as half the younger men there would be in the same boat, and there were always several girls who actually chose to come escorted only by their parents, strictly because there were so many more men they got to dance with that way. But even this knowledge failed to excite Cal; for him the dance would only be a dance were Jenny his to take. Thus he was not there when starting time rolled around that night—staying away ostensibly to roam Main Street checking the stores and saloons and to ascertain that all was peaceful throughout the rest of town—and by the time he did show up the event was already an hour under way. He found Doc Wagner in charge of checking firearms at the door, and almost without thinking began unbuckling his own gunbelt.

"You don't have to do that, Cal," the doctor said. "You're the marshal, remember?"

Cal finished unbuckling the belt. "Nobody else in there has one, do they?"

"No," the older man said thoughtfully. "I guess they don't at that." He smiled, scribbled Cal's name on a little tag that he then slipped inside the holster, and hung the gunbelt on a rack behind him. "Thanks, Cal."

Inside he found the dance floor filled. A three-piece orchestra played loudly from a portable stand installed at the opposite end of the room. Chairs lined the walls and at the moment held mostly the older members of the crowd. In a rear room, he knew, sleeping children could be found, and on a long table just to his right lay a huge pile of coats, blankets, and hats. He went over and shed his own sheepskin and Stetson, then leaned against the wall to watch.

He couldn't spot Jenny nor her escort, but others he knew were quite visible: Little Mike Wonderly and Cora Usery, Roque Gutierrez and Celsa Jaramillo, Caleb and Martha Harvey, Jeremy Chance and his wife, Gracie, Bay and Mrs. Calhoun, Lige Martin's youngest son and Frank Simpson's only daughter. . . . The list could go on and on, and there seemed nothing but happy faces among them.

Presently the music stopped and the men led their partners off the floor. Caleb Harvey came straight across the room toward Cal.

"Thought you weren't going to show up," the newspaperman said.

"I considered it," Cal replied, a bit sadly.

"Jenny's here."

Cal shrugged. "I haven't seen her. She was coming with Quentin Usery, last I heard."

"Over there," Caleb said, nodding. "They're standing beside the bandstand, talking with Jeremy and Gracie."

He saw them then, standing side-by-side and seemingly engrossed in the conversation they were having with the Chances. At least Quentin was. Jenny seemed to be looking around as if for someone. Suddenly she was looking his and Caleb's way. For a moment Cal thought she was going to wave; her free hand came up ever so slightly and was poised uncertainly for an instant before dropping quickly back to her side.

Caleb was saying, "I see Clayt Usery and his wife came to the dance separately. Guess they're not getting on so good lately, huh?"

Cal caught sight of Clayt standing across the room talking to Mel Cole, then spotted Cora a second later, sitting between Frank Simpson's wife and Celsa Jaramillo along the opposite wall. Cora seemed to be visiting amicably with Mrs. Simpson.

"Any idea what's happened between them?" Caleb went on, his interest a seemingly natural rather than a pressing one.

Cal shrugged. He had no intention of betraying any confidences and doubted that Caleb would knowingly ask him to. "Just one of those things, I reckon. Who knows?"

"Cora's still running the restaurant over at the hotel, though," Caleb continued. "Must not have been an unfriendly break."

"I don't know, Caleb. It's a hard thing to read, it really is."

Caleb said an odd thing then, considering the way he'd always seemed to feel about the Userys. "Well, for Clayt's sake, I hope it's not permanent. He needs a good woman to tide him over whatever it is that's bothered him lately. Be a shame if she can't do it for him."

Cal cast a keen gaze on the editor. "You know, Caleb, you're the second man in the past two days who's said something like that to me. It's beginning to make me wonder about a few things."

Caleb looked slightly puzzled. "Oh? What did I say? You mean about him needing a good woman?"

Cal nodded. "That, and the fact that something's been bothering him. Jeremy Chance even insists it's changed him, made him less in charge of his own interests. And Jeremy implied it was something that's come about in the past year or so." He could have gone on to relate the additional similarities with the conversation he had had with Cora, but he didn't. It was one of those confidences he didn't feel right divulging.

"Well, I guess that proves it's not just me seeing things. But I'm still not sure what you're getting at."

"Men don't change that noticeably unless there's a reason, Caleb."

"And you've just gotta know that reason."

"Is it some kind of secret?"

Caleb gave him a thoughtful look. "If it is, I don't know what it is, Cal. I really don't." For a second or two he rubbed his chin in that same thoughtful manner; then he seemed to jerk as someone began stomping a rhythmic foot from the bandstand. Presently the music struck up for another hoedown and as couples began moving back onto the floor, he began stretching his neck to see over the crowd.

"I promised Martha I wouldn't sit this one out, Cal," he explained. "Excuse me, will you?"

Cal said, "Sure," then watched as the other man made his way across the room toward his wife and thus effectively cut off a subject Cal would have liked very much to pursue. He wasn't surprised, though; he'd long since given up learning anything the easy way. With a sigh he let his gaze wander over the crowd, and presently he espied a lone figure still sitting against one wall. After only a moment's indecision, he went over and asked Cora Usery to dance.

2

Little Mike Wonderly watched as Cal swung Cora onto the dance floor. There was no malice in him because of it— he had no reason for that—but there was jealousy. Directed not just at Cal, or Cal and Cora, but at every man over five feet tall and every reasonably pretty woman in the room. At every courting young couple, at every married couple, at every *normal*-looking person he saw . . . at just about everybody, in fact.

A bachelor by anything but his own choice, Little Mike had never had a serious girl of his own. He was too short and was anything but good-looking. A little boy, he thought; at thirty-three years of age, he still looked like a homely, buck-toothed little boy. Except for Lydia Martin, he had been forced to look up at every woman he'd danced with to-night, and even Lydia was no shorter than he was. To a one they danced with him and laughed with him like he was a younger brother, a harmless child whom no girl could ever take seriously.

It was a pretty miserable feeling, for God! how he wanted them to see him as the healthy, virile man he thought he was! How he wanted and needed a woman—not just any woman, but one he could ask to be his wife, someone to share a life with, someone more than Abronia Garcia, who had her own little business after hours at the California;

someone more than the McGuire woman, who had died last year and who had never been that good anyway. . . .

So he came to the dances—had never missed one, in fact— ever hoping that one day the right girl for him would somehow appear. But tonight had been no exception to all that had gone before: There were no new girls, none he hadn't danced with many times before. And although there were several who had come unescorted, not a one of them showed more than a polite, passing interest in the little man who was the town butcher. Not one.

Even more deeply than ever before, it depressed him; created a real despondency in him, a hopelessness that for the first time seemed incurable. It not only caused him to want to leave early, but also somehow he didn't even feel like a trip to Abronia's back door, or to the bar at the saloon, where he would probably be teased for leaving the dance so soon. Home, just home. At least there he had a bottle, which he could drink alone and in peace, and which might dull his weary discouragement with it all. . . .

For a few moments more he watched the crowd on the floor, then he turned and went over to the long table where he had left his coat. It took him a moment to find it, then, hatless as usual, he donned the coat and headed for the door.

Only Doc Wagner seemed to see him go, and that only because passing the gun-check rack was unavoidable and the doc had nowhere else to sit while manning the arsenal left in his care but right beside the door. Mike never carried a gun, and to the older man's questioning stare he simply mumbled, "Not feeling too good, Doc. Think I'll sleep the rest of the night off," and passed on outside. The doc wagged his head in sad, knowing silence and watched him go.

Out front the schoolyard was filled with wagons and saddle horses, but as Mike stood on the porch and marveled at how intensely cold the air had already become, he realized there were no people outside. In summer, he knew, half a dozen couples would have drifted out by now, spooning behind a tree or a wagon, or the corner of the schoolhouse itself. Others, cowhands mostly, might be shuffling back and forth for a drink of whiskey, and a few might even have wandered off toward the saloons. But tonight the yard remained empty except for the horses and wagons.

After a moment Mike stepped down off the porch, coat collar pulled up around his neck and ears and his hands in his pockets. He shuffled between the wagons toward Main Street, to the boardwalk that began at the *Myriad* office and led from there upstreet. Lost in thought, he passed the first boardinghouse, the hotel, the doc's house, the Pioneer Saloon, then left the boardwalk on the narrow muddy road that cut behind the assay office and crossed the arroyo leading in the direction of the Victorio Mine a few miles away.

Beyond the dim lights of the saloon windows it was almost pitch dark, and he found his way as much by habit as by sight. He paid no attention to the scattering of house lights across the arroyo; they were of no interest to him, except for the fact that his own darkened cabin sat well beyond the last of them, across the road and hidden in the night.

It wasn't until he crossed the arroyo bridge that the feeling of something unusual about it all struck him. It caused him to halt momentarily and look around. He didn't know what he was looking for, but he couldn't help stopping, peering hard into the darkness ahead and then, as the feeling persisted, all around.

Behind him and to his right, light still shone from the back of the Chinaman's restaurant where the Chinaman himself lived. Forward and to his left, about fifty yards, there was a house with lighted windows. Farther along the road and again to the left, another house, but this time darkened—a bare outline against the backdrop of the wooded hillside beyond. And farther up yet, more pitch blackness, where he knew Bay Calhoun's house sat—the whole family at the dance, he told himself. Up the hill and across the road from Calhoun's sat Mike's own house, isolated and without light, impossible to make out at this distance. And finally there was the ridgetop vaguely etched against a star-studded skyline. No more houses, no more lights. And if there was anything out of the ordinary, he could not see it. . . .

But he had felt something, he knew he had. The only question was: What? A premonition? Something out there in the dark?

Suddenly he was shivering, he assumed from the intense cold, for his feet were becoming numb and his nose and ears were almost to the point of hurting. He felt foolish standing there like he was—like a child needing the bathroom but afraid to traverse the dark stretch of path that led to the privy.

"You're a fool, Mike Wonderly," he told himself. "A sure-'nough nickel-plated fool."

He walked steadily until he reached the path that led up to his front gate, but then realized that the feeling was there again and stopped once more. This time it was more intense, causing him to stare hard at the house. He could see clearly the pitch of the roof, the yawning darkness of the front porch, the picket fence that enclosed the yard . . . but nothing out of place. Nothing.

He looked behind him, then to the left and right. Still nothing. And he could hear nothing; not even a soft breeze soughing in the pinetops nearby.

He was through the gate and almost to the first step of the porch when at last he did hear—the soft sucking sound of footsteps in the mud, the unmistakable creak of saddle leather . . . coming from off to his left. Alarmed, he whirled, then blinked his eyes as the ghostly shape of a rider and his mount rounded the corner of the house. He blinked again, and his eyes became transfixed on the animal, on the just-discernible white markings and long ears of what he could only conclude was a very oddly colored mule. . . .

The rider's voice was as deep and foreboding as the little butcher's was muted. "It's been a long time, Mike. A long, long time."

3

Cal stood alone on the front porch of the schoolhouse. In the darkness before him, three cowhands had just disappeared, braving the cold in search of the saddlebags in which they had left their bottle the last trip outside. He could still hear them laughing and swearing at one another, but could no longer see them. Offhandedly, he sort of hoped they didn't find the bottle. More realistically, he knew they either would find it or they would simply go to the saloon and buy another just like it. There was no avoiding the inevitable. Even a temporary lawman learned that after a while.

He rolled a cigarette and lit it, choosing to ignore the fact that the music had started up again inside. Suddenly a light rustle and the very definite sensation of someone almost as tall as he was coming to his side caused him to turn. He was startled to find that it was Jenny.

"I should think you would be freezing, standing out here without a coat like this," she said matter-of-factly, folding and rubbing her arms briskly. "Aren't you?"

He looked at her in something akin to frustration. She wore a white sleeveless dress with yellow bodice and waist, and she looked gorgeous in it. The kind of thing calculated to make a man eat his heart out, he supposed . . . and successful as hell, too. God, how pretty she looked!

But he wouldn't tell her that; he'd be damned if he would. He only said, "At least I have sleeves on, and I needed a smoke. What's your excuse?"

Her hazel eyes shone even in the half dark. "Do I need one?"

"You're bound to have one."

She sighed and nodded her head. "You've been avoiding me again. I want to know why."

"You came with another man. I wasn't avoiding you; I just didn't want to impose." It sounded a little lame even to him.

She held his gaze like a bolt in a vise. "You're a liar, Cal. You're letting me have it and you know it. You could have asked me for a dance anytime."

He flipped his cigarette far out into the night and watched its sparks bounce off of the ground. "I figured you'd just as soon dance with him," he said.

Her eyebrows seemed to arch slightly. "Oh you did, did you? Well, what if you figured wrong? Did you ever consider that?"

It was an admission of sorts, but he did not immediately choose to acknowledge it as such. "You still came with him instead of me," he said stubbornly.

"Only because, you goose, *he* had already asked me and *I* had already accepted. What would you have me do—tell him I changed my mind in favor of someone who asked me later?"

"Something like that, yeah."

"Oh Cal . . . you wouldn't have me be that way. Surely you wouldn't."

"I'd have you be any way you have to be to stay away from Quentin Usery."

She frowned, shaking her head. "I don't think that very fair, Cal. I mean, if you're trying to demean Quentin's character . . ."

"Quentin's character doesn't need me to demean it," he said stoutly. "Believe me; I'm serious, Jenny. I don't think you know what kind of a man he is."

Again she shook her head, impatiently this time. "Maybe

I don't, but I don't need anyone else to tell me, either. I've had enough of that from Uncle Caleb. Besides, I didn't come out here to talk about him."

"Then why did you come out here? Just to express your displeasure with me for not having asked you to dance?"

"Well, yes, but . . ."

"And I suppose you think that *is* fair to your escort, huh?" He couldn't help the biting sarcasm in his words, despite the fact that he suspected he had gone too far.

She stared at him incredulously for a long moment, and finally her shoulders slumped hopelessly as she said, "I give up on you, Cal Sawyer! I really do!" Then she turned sharply toward the door and would have left him standing there had she not found her way blocked by Quentin Usery, who suddenly appeared in the doorway, a dark look on his face and anger in his eyes. "I've been looking all over for you," he said coldly.

Jenny seemed surprised at both his tone and his expression. "Why, Quentin . . . I—I was only . . ."

"I can see well enough what you were doing," he said, his anger barely under control. "So can everyone else, damn you!"

Still taken aback, Jenny stammered, "But I wasn't . . . I—I mean . . . we weren't . . . What have I done?"

"You've left the man you came to this dance with standing like a fool while you lollygag around with another out here in the dark—that's what you've done, by God!" There was an exaggerated air of indignation, but something else too . . . a certain raised pitch of voice, a wildness Cal didn't like at all.

"I'm sorry, Quentin. I—" Jenny sounded a little stiff herself now, but seemed willing to try to mollify the situation. But he didn't give her a chance; he interrupted rudely, sarcastically, "Yeah, I just bet you are, you—you . . ." He seemed not to find the right word, and for some reason his eyes for the first time came in contact with Cal's. "And you

. . . I thought I made it clear to you to lay off where Miss Bayles is concerned."

"You did what?" Jenny asked incredulously, before Cal could respond. "You told him what?" Her eyes seemed to narrow as she studied him. "Quentin Usery, if I had known you did something like that . . . I'd never have come to this dance with you! Never!" It was a plain statement that Cal realized was no longer intended to pacify.

But if Usery noticed the deeper finality of her words, he didn't let on; he simply reached out with a rough hand and grabbed her arm, yanking her toward him. "Well, you *did* come with me, and you're going to see it through whether you like it or not." He turned and began pulling her toward the door.

"Just a minute, Usery!" Cal said sharply as he grabbed the other man by the shoulder and whirled him around.

Usery glared at him. "Lay off, Sawyer!"

"When you let go of the girl, I will," Cal said.

"When I'm ready, damn you. When I'm ready and not a minute sooner. Now butt out, you hear?"

Once more he turned, hauling the still resisting but otherwise helpless girl with him, and once again Cal grabbed him by the shoulder.

Somehow the man whirled around differently this time, more on his own and with a greater force. Cal would tell himself later that he should have known, should have been ready. But he wasn't. He saw the fist blurring his way in the same instant he heard Jenny scream. Light rocketed through his head as the blow smashed like a hammer into his mouth and he felt himself hurtling backward, tumbling and rolling down the porch, and Jenny was still screaming. From inside the schoolhouse someone was yelling, "Fight! Fight!" and a rush of footsteps and excited voices followed close behind.

Cal started up the steps after Usery but got only partway before a heavy boot came sailing toward his head. He ducked, caught the foot with one hand, and held it against his shoulder as he fell backward once more. Both men tumbled down the steps to the ground, Usery cursing and thrashing, Cal trying to avoid being kicked and thinking hard about regaining his feet before his opponent did.

He managed to do just that, but only in time to unsuccessfully ward off a lunging tackle that took them both to the ground again. Cal wound up on bottom, and before he knew how it had happened was receiving a wild pummeling about the head and shoulders. Somehow, in his desperation to get loose, he made a violent twist that threw Usery to the side and allowed Cal to roll away and get to his feet. Again the other man came in a crouching lunge, but this time Cal was in a position to sidestep and swing, catching his attacker with a crunching right to the side of the head.

Usery went sprawling with a crash against the porch steps and lay there as if stunned, shaking his head and drawing hoarse breaths. Cal, only dimly aware of the crowd that had come spilling out to surround them, stood there like a fool and let his man get up.

"Okay . . . you bastard," Usery panted, raising his hands and coming to a prize fighter's stance. "Try this!" He moved in quickly, feinting, then jabbing, then swinging hard with a right to the ribs.

But Cal was no longer at a disadvantage; he had probably had two fights in his life to Usery's one, and he was quite willing to take at least the rib shot for another chance at the other man's head. Cal lashed out viciously with a left-and-right combination, which straightened his opponent as if stung from behind, then hooked with a left that cracked cleanly against the man's jaw. Usery went down in a heap.

"Whoopee!" someone yelled from the crowd. "That's givin' it to him, Cal!"

"Yeah! Pile on him, boy! Let him have it good!"

But Usery had rolled over, groaning, flopping then on his back as if beaten and out. Cal stood, his legs spread apart and breathing hard through smashed lips, somehow unable to do as had been called for him to do and pile on a beaten man. After a moment, he straightened and started to walk away—which should have been a predictable mistake, for before he had taken two steps a foot came out of nowhere, tripping him forward. He pitched to the ground and rolled over, realizing as he got to one knee that Usery was already on his feet. He stared helplessly as the man aimed another kick his way.

But it was never delivered; from out of the crowd came a husky form, stout arms wrapping around Quentin Usery's shoulders and yanking him into the air, literally flinging him to the side. Then, like a stern father talking to an insufferably erring son, the second figure waded into him, cursing and backhanding, sending him whimpering to the ground.

The crowd became completely hushed as Clayt Usery stood over his fallen brother, fury exuding from his every pore. "Damn you, Quentin! Damn your fool hide! I know you started this, and I know why. I won't stand for it, you hear! I won't!"

Quentin rose slowly, wiping blood from his mouth and nose. For a long moment he stood there, his breath a rasping wheeze, saying nothing, not needing to. His own fury was obvious even in the half light. A blazing, violent anger shone in his eyes, a sickening sight to all around who beheld what it was.

What would have happened next was anybody's guess, for it was then that Soo Lin, the Chinaman, came running up from somewhere outside the circle of the crowd. He was shouting and waving his arms, oblivious it seemed to whatever had been going on before he arrived.

"Somebody," he panted, "somebody gotta come. Gotta . . . come see. I heah gunshots . . . two, thlee times. Somebody shootin' up the hill behind my prace. . . ." He paused, looking around expectantly in wide-eyed excitement.

"Aw come on, Soo," someone said amid several laughs.

"What's a few gunshots on a Saturday night? Happens all the time, you know that."

The little Chinese shook his head vigorously. "No, no, no! Not ah da time. Not rike dis. Mebbe rike da Ra Belles, I tink. Huh? Huh?"

Suddenly, whether the Chinaman's words were logical or not, there were no more laughs, and it was Cal standing before Soo Lin. "What's up there, Soo—behind your place? Anything?"

"Way up dere . . . da load to da mine," Soo said, thinking, then adding, "Dat's all, 'cept for Ritter Mike's prace. . . ."

Cal whirled, searching the crowd. "Mike's here somewhere, isn't he? I saw him earlier."

"Not anymore, Cal," Doc Wagner said, stepping out of the crowd. "He left a little while ago. Said he didn't feel good and was going home to sleep it off. Been better'n a half hour now, I'd say."

Cal turned to face Clayt Usery. "I think I better go up there, Clayt. It may be nothing, but I think I better go see."

Usery nodded grimly and said, "I'll go with you." Then he turned and told the crowd, "Okay, we could use a couple or three men and some lanterns. The rest of you get on back inside the dance and don't worry. This deal's probably nothing, probably nothing at all."

As Cal watched the crowd begin to drift back inside, he saw Caleb with his arm around Jenny's shoulders, leading her up the porch steps, and for a vague, hurried moment he even looked around for Quentin Usery. But somehow, during the excitement, that individual seemed to have completely disappeared. With a shrug, he turned to the business at hand as a couple of volunteers and Soo Lin came forward to go with him and Usery up the hill.

SIX

USERY'S SHAME

1

For the second time in a week there was a burial at the Grafton cemetery. Only four days before it had been the double affair for the La Belle brothers, graveside services conducted by Father O'Mary of the Catholic church; today, Monday, it was for Little Mike Wonderly, presided over by the Right Reverend Nathan Gregg of the Methodists.

Little Mike, like the La Belles, had no known kin to handle the affair or even to contact, yet almost a hundred people attended his funeral. This, despite a cold, cloudy day—the dreariest by far since the snow of the week before—which not only provided a likely atmosphere for the sad event at hand but also almost certainly foreshadowed more harsh weather to come. It fit Cal Sawyer's mood, too, as the service was ended and he and Caleb walked down the hill together toward where saddle horses and buggies had been left. Most of the crowd, including Jenny and Aunt Martha, had already preceded them.

"It just doesn't make any sense, Cal," Caleb was saying for maybe the tenth time since it had happened. "Why on earth would anyone want to kill Little Mike?"

Cal wagged his head in frustration. "Why would anyone want to kill the La Belles? Why anything, in a deal like this?"

"But you do think it's one and the same person?" Caleb said.

"I'm convinced of it. Aren't you?"

"I don't know. I guess I am—at least I hope there's no more than one such crazy idiot around. But I just can't understand why . . . and I can't figure who. That's the real kicker, Cal: *Who* in hell is he?"

"I told you already who I think he is."

Caleb stopped to look Cal in the eye. "The stranger on the paint mule. You still claim those were mule tracks you found alongside the yard fence?"

"I'd swear to it. And so would some others. Ask Soo Lin, or Lige Martin. Or ask Jeremy. Nobody knows what an unshod mule foot looks like better than Jeremy."

"But you couldn't track him. You tried all morning yesterday, and even in the mud and snow you couldn't tell where he went."

"We lost the tracks on the mine road, Caleb," Cal explained patiently. "Which isn't too surprising, what with the dance breaking up and as many as five wagons and a dozen riders passing over it after he did. What really puzzled us was, he must have left the main road somewhere, and we couldn't even find where that was."

"Maybe he took one of the side roads that goes to one of the ranches," Caleb suggested. "There are at least four or five of those, you know."

"That's what we figured, too," Cal said unhappily. "But we couldn't find where he left any of those roads, either. He just disappeared, like a damn ghost or something."

Caleb's eyes were keen. "You don't really believe *that*, do you?"

Cal smiled thinly. "No, not literally—although it is tempting, believe me. But wherever he went, or whatever tracks he left . . . well, one way or another all sign of him got covered up by other tracks, either horses and wagons, or maybe even cattle. I know we found fifteen or twenty cattle trails that crossed the roads. He could have taken any of those. No way we were ever going to track him after a bunch of cows followed him. We'd be a week trying to find which trail he took and another week finding where he left it. Just no way."

"Then what are you going to do?" Caleb asked penetratingly as they began to walk again. "Surely you're not going to just give up."

Cal shook his head. "No, I won't give up. I know the man is in the country still—I figure holed up in the Black Range somewhere but still within striking distance of town. And I'm all but convinced now that he's the stranger I saw on the spotted mule the other day."

"So you're going to do what? Gather up a posse and comb the hills till you find him?"

"Something like that, yeah. Fact is, I thought I'd start getting some men lined up this afternoon, be ready to head out first thing tomorrow morning—weather permitting, of course."

Caleb's eyes lingered meaningfully on the cloudy sky overhead. "You better cross your fingers on that last, I'd say. And there's a lot of country between here and the top of the Black Range—a hundred canyons and ridges, miles long each one. From Animas Creek to Stone Canyon, south to north, and Alamosa Canyon to Round Mountain, east to west. Lots of it in timbered hills where you can't see a quarter of a mile in any direction, sometimes not even fifty yards. And if we get another snowstorm . . . well, you and I both know that fellow could stay holed up all winter with fifty men looking for him and never be found."

As they reached the foot of the hill and stopped alongside Caleb's buggy, Cal had a deep frown on his face that said he knew the other man was right in everything he said; Cal couldn't help a dismal glance of his own at the sky.

Caleb reached up and laid a hand on Cal's shoulder then. "I'm sorry, boy. I shouldn't be so discouraging. You've got to try, and what you have in mind is probably as good an angle as anybody's. Don't let what I said keep you from it."

"Thanks, Caleb," Cal said, and was just about to step away toward his grulla, standing tied to a bush a dozen or so yards away, when another voice called from inside the buggy. "Cal—just a moment, Cal. Don't go yet." It was Jenny, leaning out so he could see her sitting next to her Aunt Martha. "Please . . . I want to apologize for Saturday night."

He turned back, noticing as he did that Caleb had walked around to the other side of the buggy and was fidgeting with some harness or something there. Jenny quickly stepped down and came to him.

"Do you accept my apology?" she persisted, her eyes directly on his still swollen lips.

"It wasn't your fault," Cal said, shrugging. "It was just something that happened. You had no control over it."

"I know," she said. "But I didn't believe what you told me about Quentin Usery. I should have. And I should have gone to the dance with you instead of him. Do you forgive me?"

He looked at her for a long moment, satisfying himself of her sincerity but, strangely, taking no great pleasure in the fact as he did. "Yes, I guess so, Jenny. I don't blame you, and I don't hold grudges against pretty girls just because they won't go to dances with me."

She smiled weakly, a small sign of hope showing in her eyes, and he realized then how hard this had been for her to do. "Thank you, Cal. Maybe next dance I can make it up to you—if you should ask me again, of course." There was a good deal of honest humility in her voice as she added, "Do you think you might . . . ask me?"

"I think I might," he said, unable, in the face of her, to make her pay any more dearly than she already had.

It was apparently the right thing to say, for she suddenly

looked so relieved and happy that she seemed about to reach up and kiss him full on his bruised lips, and might have, too, but for the shuffling of her Uncle Caleb near the carriage behind her and a polite little cough from her Aunt Martha inside it.

Cal watched as she crawled back inside the buggy and a few seconds later as Caleb drove them away. But he felt only a momentary lift in spirit, one that should have lasted longer—and would have, had it not been for the first lazy flakes of snow that began falling from the sky, looking very much like relentless presages of an even worse storm than the one of almost a week ago.

2

From the start he knew there was never going to be any point to his trying to line up a posse for the next day. Even before he arrived back in town from the cemetery, the snow was swirling in dense blankets that already had begun to lay the ground white, like cream whipped to a frothy fluff, and he suspected the first storm was indeed going to be like a kitten compared to a lion in light of this one. By evening, when there was already half a foot fallen on the street in front of the jail, he knew it beyond a doubt. He crossed to the restaurant at the Manor House, hands in pockets and collar turned up, his mood made all the worse by old Enos' parting sally: "Eat good, boy. This'll close down the mines for sure, an' your appetite may go beggin' tomorrow. Hate to say it, but—" Cal had closed the door on him, neither wanting nor needing to hear any more.

Inside the restaurant, he found the evening crowd just beginning to thin out and Cora Usery taking her supper alone in a booth on the far side of the room. At a table next to her sat Roque Gutierrez and Celsa Jaramillo, apparently having just been served.

"Hello, Roque. Celsa," Cal greeted, stopping at Cora's table. "Cora."

Roque and Celsa returned his greeting in turn, and Cora said, "Have a seat, Cal. Here, with me. Marquetta will take your order in just a minute." Marquetta Gonzales was the evening waitress who usually relieved Cora sometime around five in the afternoon.

"What's good?" he asked, sliding in across from her. "Anything?"

Cora smiled. "Everything. But I'd recommend what I'm having—the special: beef stew with fresh sourdough biscuits straight from the oven. It's the quickest way to get served and the best thing in the world for the kind of weather we're having."

"Warms you up in no time, does it?" he said, with a distinctly halfhearted smile of his own. It seemed that any mention whatsoever of the weather was enough to send his spirits plunging, and it was, at this stage, all but impossible for him to hide the fact.

Cora's expression was immediately sympathetic. "Things just don't seem to be going your way lately, do they, Cal? These awful killings, the weather, that fight with Quentin Saturday night . . . I was so ashamed to learn how that started, how Quentin caused it, and then the way he fought you."

Cal's smile was again a faint one, made self-conscious by still swollen lips and a dark bruise that he knew showed plainly above his left eye. "I guess I was a little ashamed, too," he said. "Especially since I damn near got whipped for not knowing better than to turn my back on him. If it hadn't been for Clayt, I suspect I'd have gotten my teeth kicked in."

Cora looked thoughtful. "Have you seen Quentin since then?"

Cal shook his head. "Matter of fact, I haven't. Why?"

"I was just wondering. It doesn't seem that anyone else has either. Not around town, at least."

"Is that so unusual?"

"Well, it is, sort of," she said. "Especially for a Sunday and Monday. And he wasn't at Little Mike's funeral today, either. I think it's at least a little strange that he hasn't been seen at all."

It was then that Marquetta appeared at the table, and Cal ordered the special Cora had recommended. When the girl was gone, he turned back to the topic at hand. "You say Quentin hasn't been around town—maybe he went to the ranch, or even up to the mines."

Cora shook her head. "Clayt was out at the ranch all day yesterday, and he came back last night saying Quentin hadn't been seen out there in over a week. And the mines are closed on Sunday. No one up there except the guards, and Clayt talked to one of them this morning: still no sign of Quentin. No sign anywhere."

Cal thought about this for a moment and finally shrugged. "I suspect he's probably off sulking somewhere. I battered his face a little bit and Clayt battered his pride probably a lot. I imagine he'll show up in a day or two. He's not going to leave the territory just because of that one incident."

Cora didn't look relieved. "I think that's what bothers me, Cal. He probably is sulking, maybe worse than that even, and he's certainly not the kind to forget or forgive a thing like that. I'm really afraid of what he might do when he does come back."

Somehow Cal knew she was probably right to feel this way, although he didn't know just how much worry it should cause him personally. If Quentin Usery was bound and determined to hold a grudge, it seemed more likely its most bitter angle would be directed toward his brother Clayt. Cal didn't think he would ever forget the look of anger, and maybe even hatred, he'd seen on Quentin's face after Clayt had manhandled him so. This alone caused him to understand much of Cora's concern.

After a moment, he asked, "Is Clayt in town?"

Cora nodded. "He went to the funeral, then stayed in town when the storm settled in. He ate here about an hour ago and left for the house. I'm sure he'll stay in tomorrow to see if the mines will have to be closed down because of the snow."

It was then that Marquetta reappeared, this time with a steaming bowl of stew, a plate of biscuits, and a fresh serving of butter and honey, which caused Cal to realize for the first time how really hungry he was.

"I guess this weather has put a crimp in your plans to try and hunt down Mike Wonderly's killer," Cora commented presently as she finished her own meal.

"No question about that," Cal said. "Not much point trying to take a posse out in something like this anyway, and worse, now, we've got no chance of picking up the guy's tracks again."

"I heard you think it was the man on the spotted mule. The one you thought might be Guthrie McGuire."

Cal eyed her with some amazement. "News sure gets around," he said. "But yes, I do think that may be who it is —the man on the mule. At least I'm convinced whoever killed Mike did ride a mule. I have no evidence besides the tracks found at the scene and certainly nothing to definitely tie to McGuire. That's still speculation only I seem inclined toward, I'm afraid."

"Have you learned any more about the man? Anything that might make him want to kill not only the La Belles, but Little Mike as well?"

"No," he said. "And I haven't been able to learn any more about his wife either. People seem to clam up the minute either of them is mentioned. Either they really don't know anything, or they won't tell, I can't figure out which. It's about the same when I go to asking what's been bothering

Clayt the past year or so. Several people, including yourself, have said there has been something, but again, no one can say what. I've even begun wondering if there's some connection between him and the McGuires. I'm not sure why, but I really do wonder."

Cora had a concerned look on her face that made him wonder if maybe she hadn't had the same thought. But all she said was, "I wish I knew, Cal—for my own sake as well as yours. It might mean a lot to my marriage if I did."

Cal started to say something to this, but suddenly became aware that Roque and Celsa had risen from their table and were preparing to leave. "See you, Cal. Cora," Roque said. Cal said "Good night," then noticed that Celsa, who had said nothing other than to nod politely, had a strangely serious expression on her face, which caused him to wonder how much of his and Cora's conversation she might have overheard.

He watched them leave, then told Cora, "Well, the stew was good and so was the company, but it's dark out now and someone's got to make the rounds of the street."

Cora smiled weakly. "Even on a night like this? I do believe you must be taking to your new job, Cal. You really must."

He smiled back, knowing that she damn well knew better. "Good night, Cora," he said, and headed across the room to sign out.

It was at the door that Marquetta Gonzales handed him the note, a folded piece of paper with his name written on the outside in a clear feminine script that he somehow knew was not Marquetta's.

"It's from Señorita Jaramillo," the girl told him. "She said I should not tell anyone else I gave it to you and that you should read it outside. She said there was something you should know."

Cal, never doubting that Celsa's standing among the Mexican community of Grafton would guarantee her sealed lips from Marquetta, stepped out into the parlor and unfolded the note. It read:

Cal, I hope you will forgive my boldness, but will you come to my room behind the dress shop in about an hour? As to the reason, please suffice it to say that I, too, have seen the man on the spotted mule!

Celsa

3

Cal didn't know everything there was to know about Celsa Jaramillo, but he did know that she came from an old Spanish family down Socorro way, and that she was in no way the typical dusky *señorita* whose only pattern of life was, some thought, to learn to bat her eyes by age thirteen, marry by sixteen or seventeen, and breed prolifically until thirty-five or -six, by which time she would turn to fat and become a sharp-tongued old hen who would drive her husband out of the house so regularly and viciously that he would be called a fool for ever coming back. Cal, himself, thought this less typical than striking anyway, and certainly could not see Celsa falling into such a style. Sure, she could bat eyes with the best of them, and, although several years past sixteen, would probably marry someday. But she was also bright, industrious, able to command her own way in the local business realm, and better educated somehow than a good many of the Anglo girls he'd known.

Not only this, she also had lived in Grafton practically since its inception, was well respected, and knew, or had known, almost everyone who had ever lived there. And she had seen the man on the spotted mule! This simple declaration had both so excited and intrigued Cal that the hour after he left the hotel dragged by as if it were a month. Throughout his rounds of the street he was almost completely distracted by questions as to what it might mean. What had she overheard in his and Cora's conversation that made her want to talk with him? Had she recognized the man on the mule? Did she know who he was? Surely she hadn't suspected him to be McGuire; else why hadn't she said something before? After all, it wasn't every day that a dead man rode through town! And what about Roque? He must have overheard everything Celsa did. Did he know anything? Cal even hunted for Gutierrez as he checked in on the California, but did not find him there and could not learn where he was.

It was shortly after eight and still snowing when he calculated that the hour was finally up, without once wondering why Celsa had not said sooner, for there could have been any number of good reasons for that. He sauntered from the jail the hundred or so feet to Celsa's dress shop, then stood on the boardwalk for several seconds, making sure that no one was around who might see him duck into the alley that led to the back of the shop. After a moment, he turned the corner and approached Celsa's door. He knocked lightly.

"Who's there?" It was Celsa, being cautious.

"Cal—Cal Sawyer."

The door cracked partway and Celsa's face appeared in the opening. Quickly she stepped back and let him through, then closed the door behind him. Motioning to a chair nearby, she said, "I wasn't sure you'd come, Cal . . . but I'm very glad you did."

Cal looked around and found the room modestly though not meagerly furnished, a combined living and cooking area with hearth and fireplace, fire ablaze on one side, a high-backed cowhide sofa and chair across from it, a crudely built set of cabinets for dishes and utensils, a dim portrait of the Christ on one wall, and a large crucifix hanging above an oil lamp and stand nearby. A door next to this apparently led into the abode's lone bedroom. He hung his hat and coat on a rack beside the door and moved over to the chair.

Celsa said, "I hope you don't mind my being so secretive. Do you think anyone saw you come? I mean . . . I haven't told Roque, and I'm not sure how easy it would be to explain. . . ."

Cal grinned understandingly. Already during the past week he had been invited into a pretty woman's room, at night, coming and going in a clandestine fashion—albeit for purely proper reasons—and now here he was again: another woman, another room, but under what appeared to be distinctly similar circumstances. And yet, how hard to explain if he was seen.

"I'm really not all that practiced at slipping in and out of pretty ladies' rooms," he told her, continuing to smile, "but I think I made it undetected this time. I tried, anyway."

She smiled back, as if to say, "Thank you," and then asked, "Would you like some coffee? I have a pot on the fire."

Cal allowed that he would and watched as she took out two cups and poured them full. Handing him his, she then took a seat on the sofa across from him. "Well, I guess you want to know why I was listening in on your conversation with Cora. I am sorry about that, Cal. I wasn't trying to—at least at first."

"Until you heard me say something about the man on the spotted mule," he suggested expectantly.

She shrugged. "Mostly then, I guess—when Cora mentioned the name of Guthrie McGuire, and you indicated you had not only been trying to find out about him but his dead wife too. It really hit me—that you even knew about them, much less that you were somehow connecting them with the killings."

"Why? Because you thought them both dead?"

She looked at him keenly. "Because I *knew* they were both dead, Cal. At least I thought I did." She smiled as he once again gave her an expectant look. "Yes—until I remembered seeing the man on the mule. But don't misunderstand.

I still find it hard to believe Guthrie McGuire is not dead. And his wife, Cassie, died in my arms, so there is no question there. But I am curious, Cal; and unless I find out more about your suspicions, I'll think my mind is playing tricks on me forever about that fellow on the mule."

"Why?" Cal asked, having a tremendous time trying to hold back his excited curiosity. "When did you see him? Did he *look* like Guthrie McGuire?"

She looked indecisive. "I suppose I saw him the same time you did—last week, the day of the first snow. He rode straight through town and disappeared going in the direction of the mines. Is that when you saw him?" She paused as Cal nodded, then went on. "As to who he looked like, I didn't think about it at the time, of course, since he is supposed to be dead . . . but yes, he did resemble McGuire. The beard and clothing were different, but the man . . ." She looked at him very seriously. "Cal, what made you even think about McGuire? Is it really possible he's not dead? What is it you know?"

Cal frowned, somewhat discouraged that *she* should be asking *him* this. "The trouble is, I'm not sure I know anything. In fact, it may be as wild a stab as I've ever taken at anything. It all started with something Clayt Usery said, then something about the stranger on the mule, things others said, something about the La Belle murders—and now Little Mike's as well—that caused me to conjecture about a man who might hold a grudge against people in this town. It's a lot of guesswork and really nothing much more, I'm afraid. Maybe nothing at all."

But Celsa, surprisingly, did not look discouraged. "I'm not so sure about that yet, Cal," she said. "Tell me more about what Clayton Usery told you. Tell me what things others said that caused you to conjecture so. Tell me everything you can think of—then we'll see whether it's nothing or not."

Cal studied her for a long moment; then, still only cautiously optimistic, he thought back to the beginning and began telling her everything he knew.

A short while later, when he had finished, Celsa said, "Well, I have no idea if it's really possible for Guthrie McGuire to still be alive. I know I certainly wouldn't think so—*if* I hadn't seen that man on the mule. . . ." She looked at him with what seemed an almost fatalistic air. "But I did see him, Cal; and he did look like McGuire. And believe me, if ever a man had reason to want revenge, he's the one. Very few people know that, but it's true. More so than you might guess, believe me."

"You knew his wife," Cal said, suddenly remembering. "You said she died in your arms. Were you friends? Is that how you know about McGuire?"

She nodded—he thought sadly. "I was probably Cassie McGuire's only *real* friend. She never had a very high standing among the ladies of the town, but after her husband was sent off to prison, well, I won't say she was exactly ostracized, but she didn't have any real friends, and she was so ashamed of what had happened that I guess she couldn't bring herself to try to make any. Even I had to go out of my way to befriend her, and still there was only me . . . and the men. I don't know what you would call them, but I don't think it would be friends."

Cal frowned. "Men? What men? You mean she . . . ?"

Celsa nodded. "It was very sad, Cal. She was so alone, so lost. She had no money, no job, nowhere to go. She was a strange person. Very humble and yet proud, too. Too proud to take a job in my dress shop because she thought it charity —which it would have been, I guess, and low-paying at that."

"Were there . . . a lot of men?" Cal asked, trying to visualize how pathetic the situation must have been.

A mildly troubled look came across Celsa's face then as she thought about it. "For a time, I guess there were quite a few. I don't really know how it started. She lived in a small house across the arroyo and she worked for a couple of weeks in the Pioneer Saloon, right after it was built. It may have started there. No question it grew enough that she finally developed quite a business—and a reputation to go with it. Almost everyone knew about her, but what few did know is that she eventually came to be kept by one man, a situation that I believe also led to her death. . . ." She caught Cal's abrupt look of interest and suddenly seemed regretful. She went on to explain, "I knew about it because I was a friend, Cal. And it has always been a secret well kept. I—I'm not sure I should have told you that at all. . . ."

"Because of the man," he said, instantly perceptive. "Surely that poor dead woman had nothing left to hide. Does the man still live here? Do I know him? Is that the reason?"

"It's part of it, Cal. But there is more. Toward the end there was another man—which was an even better-kept secret than the first. I have never told anyone either of their names, and I am almost sure no one else knew of the second man."

Cal hardly knew what to say to this, and after a moment's pause, Celsa went on, "I know. I know. I said she came to be kept by one man. And she did. A man who loved her sincerely. But there *was* another man—unknown to the first, of course—who lured her and used her unmercifully, fascinated her, practically—how would you say—hypnotized her? Yes—like a snake a rabbit. And in the end it was he who drove her to the ultimate in shame and guilt. Literally destroyed what little there was left of her to destroy."

Intrigued, Cal asked, "How did she die?"

Celsa wagged her head. "She became violently ill one night, very suddenly and without warning, and died a short while later. It was I who found her and sent for Doc Wagner, although there was nothing he could do when he got there. He finally gave a diagnosis of food poisoning, but he never really seemed very sure of that. For my part I will always believe she knowingly took something that would cause her death. I believe she wanted to die."

"Was there any evidence of that?"

She shrugged. "I found a cup beside her bed, empty but still containing the residue of something she must have drank not long before I found her. It was very bad-smelling, not like anything you would drink for pleasure or to quench your thirst. It seemed like pretty good evidence to me, even though no one ever really knew what it was."

"Didn't Doc Wagner know?"

"He said he didn't," she said. "And he had no way to find out. He seemed to prefer to think it some kind of home remedy she had learned somewhere. Something she'd taken when she first became ill." She shrugged then. "Who knows? Maybe he's right. There are hundreds of such concoctions, especially among my people and the Indians. Maybe that's what it was."

"But you still don't think so," Cal said. "You think she took her life, driven to it by this man who had so used her. . . ." He paused, thinking, wondering if anything about this connected with anything else. Suddenly a thought struck him. "Celsa, is it possible Guthrie McGuire could have learned what happened to his wife from his prison cell in Santa Fe? Maybe not all the details, but enough. Enough to cause him to break out of prison and come back here?"

Celsa was looking at him sympathetically, but without encouragement. "What about his so-called death, Cal? He was seen up near Las Vegas before it happened, his body identified. If he was bent on coming back here for revenge, why would he go there? Why would he let all this time pass?"

Cal shook his head. "I don't know for sure, but I do know that the man killed near Las Vegas was mauled by a bear— 'beyond recognition,' according to the account I saw. He was identified as Guthrie McGuire strictly on the basis of his clothing and sightings reported a few days before. Who knows? Maybe the whole thing is some crazy mistake. Maybe McGuire never was around Las Vegas. . . . Who knows, Celsa?"

She held her coffee cup between two hands, looking slightly incredulous but at the same time appearing not quite able to disbelieve.

He went on. "Celsa, listen. Assuming I'm right. Assuming there is a way—and believe me, there are ways—McGuire could have learned any of what you've told me from his prison cell. Assuming, even, he might somehow have learned the name of either of his wife's lovers. Oh I know, a well-kept secret—but I don't think we can take anything for granted here, now. I think we have to assume he may have known at least of the first man and possibly even the second." He paused. "Celsa, I'm charged with law and order around this town right now, and because of it am up to my neck in these killings. I'm not only determined to try to bring the guilty party to ground, but I'm also desperate to avoid any more deaths. I've got to protect people any way I can, and you've got to tell me who those two men are."

Celsa actually squirmed. "Oh Cal—please! I—I don't know. I'm not sure. . . ."

"What is it? Are you afraid?"

She nodded very slightly, but said, "Not of the first man . . . the second. I am very afraid of the second." She looked at him unhappily. "Oh Cal, must I? Must I tell?"

He gave her a long, sympathetic look. "I'm sorry, Celsa. I would never ask if I didn't think it necessary. But I've got to know. I've got to know who he might shoot next. Who was the man who kept Cassie McGuire?"

She dropped her head, and then very quietly said, "He's a good man, Cal. He never knew about the other man, and he has not been happy. He doesn't deserve to have this thing come completely into the open."

"I understand," Cal said. "I only want to protect him. I don't want to drag his name through the mud." Then, having divined a good deal now, and not wanting to make it any harder for her than it already was, he asked, "Was it Clayton Usery?"

She nodded in the affirmative. "I think at first he only felt sorry for Cassie. But later I think—no, I'm sure—he really loved her. And I think she loved him. He might even have been her salvation if she had been able to resist the other man. . . ." She stopped suddenly, as if stricken with the certain inevitability of what had to come next. It seemed to disturb her immensely, so much so that Cal felt obliged to reconsider his own determined desire to know, to make her tell the second man's name.

He said, "I won't force you, Celsa. If you don't want to say. . . ."

She met his gaze, and for a moment held it indecisively. Then something in her demeanor changed, relaxed. She said, "No. It would be wrong for me not to now. I would only be protecting him, and he has never deserved that." A hard light came into her eyes then. "It was Quentin Usery, Cal—Clayt's own brother."

For a moment he simply stared at her, unable any longer to find anything much of a surprise. Finally he asked, "Did Quentin know about his brother and Cassie McGuire? You said Clayt didn't know there was another man, but did Quentin?"

"Oh yes," she said bitterly. "He knew. There was never any doubt in my mind that he knew. The bastard."

Although somehow not startled by the epithet at all, Cal could still only shake his head. "He knew . . . and yet he—"

Celsa didn't let him finish. "He knew, Cal. From the beginning. He knew every moment of the way. He knew what he was doing to Cassie, and he knew what it would finally do to his brother if Clayt ever found out. He knew all of that, and yet he still did what he did."

"Good lord!" Cal said, hardly able to believe. "How could anybody . . . ?"

Celsa met his gaze somberly, knowingly. "That's just the kind of man Quentin is, Cal. The kind of man he is."

4

It was in more than just a petulant sulk that the subject of these remarks had disappeared from town two nights before. The depth of the bitterness inside him would have been impossible to measure, even then, before he had ridden all day aimlessly up into the Black Range, up one canyon and down another, thinking, brooding, his half-crazed desire for revenge against those who had humiliated him tempered only by some remnant of sanity, which insisted that whatever he was to do must be done covertly; that he was not yet ready to sacrifice all for revenge alone. And he was stumped by this, for he could think of no plan that would avoid it. He rode and rode, and still could not think of one.

He camped Sunday night along the banks of what would someday be called Taylor Creek, in the shivering cold of high mountain air, with only a tiny campfire and two light blankets to keep him warm. He slept little and thought a lot. And he decided nothing, except that he would not go back to Grafton, not yet.

He needed some place to stay, some place isolated where he could be completely alone. He had a few supplies— enough to get him by for three or four days, enough to get him settled in. After that he could worry about replenishing his pack. The thing now was: Where to go? Over a small breakfast fire and a hot cup of coffee the next morning he decided at least that. Less than an hour later he saddled up —his favorite horse, a dark bay with unmarked face and black feet all around—and rode out beneath a sky already clouded over, angling uphill and slightly to the north, moving ever higher into the Black Range.

It took until almost noon for him to find it: the now long-abandoned cabin of an old prospector killed by Apaches in 1883. He had been to it more than once and had ridden the country around it several times. The rumor was—and it had persisted ever since the prospector's death—that the old guy had found a rich gold vein somewhere nearby, a possibility that the Usery Mining Company, represented by Quentin Usery, had been more than a little interested in pursuing. Trouble was, no one had ever found a thing, and although the rumor held on, active searching had died down to an inconsistent dribble. Until now, when almost nobody passed this way anymore and the prospector's cabin had become as unfrequented as any place around.

Nevertheless, even having been to it more than once, Quentin had trouble toward the last finding the right canyon, the spring-fed creek that ran close by, the cabin itself. And by the time he did, a few flakes of snow had already begun to float earthward, causing him to be less than careful in his hurry to reach shelter. When he came riding somewhat carelessly out of a thick stand of pine into the opening that held the cabin, he was surprised and not just a little dismayed to see smoke coming from the chimney. Collecting himself quickly, he reined the bay back into the trees, then worked his way around to a point where he could get a good view without being seen.

He had just begun to study the house when a movement in the corral out back caught his eye. There was an animal there . . . a horse. A paint horse, it seemed. Or was it? He squinted to get a better look. It was snowing harder now, restricting his vision just enough so he could not tell.

But he had to know. Suddenly he had remembered his conversation with Cal Sawyer last week in front of the jail: the talk of a man who might have had something to do with the killings of Jess and Hiram La Belle; a man who had

caused Sawyer to be awfully interested in one Guthrie Mc-
Guire, who everyone thought dead; a stranger who had ridden through town on a *spotted mule!* And Quentin Usery had
seen that stranger ride through and had not thought of
McGuire . . . until Sawyer started asking questions. Questions that made one stop and think back on what one man
looked like and then the other. It had been disturbing then
and was even more disturbing now.

Slowly he dismounted and tied the bay to a nearby bush,
then carefully began moving through brush just tall enough
that he could keep himself screened from the cabin. After a
minute or two he had worked himself to a spot within fifty
yards of the small enclosure. Snow was coming down heavily now and he almost couldn't see the cabin, much less the
animal penned behind it. There was no longer any brush to
hide behind, but he figured anyone looking his way would
be just as visually handicapped as he was now, so he crept
low and began moving closer.

Presently he was to a point where he could see that there
were no windows along the cabin's back wall, and after a
brief moment's consideration he felt it safe to dash toward
it. In about ten quick strides he was standing with his back
to the wall, breathing hard—and staring directly at the animal in the corral. As if he needed any confirmation now that
it was a mule—a chestnut and white-marked mare with the
unmistakable long flop ears and tan muzzle of its hybrid
breed—the thing abruptly let out a loud, long bray. Almost
immediately a hopeful nicker came from out of the snow-
filled air from but a short distance away, and Usery flattened himself even closer against the wall. It had been his
bay answering, and it was that which he knew might give
his presence away.

Instinctively he drew his six-gun and stood breathlessly
still, trying hard to hear if anyone was stirring inside the
cabin and praying that neither the mule nor the horse would
make another sound. His heart almost stopped as he heard a

door creak open from around the corner and, a few moments later, a low curse from whoever had opened it.

For a brief few seconds he considered making a run for cover, but then realized that he was too far away from anything. He heard a noise like a footfall from just around the opposite corner of the cabin; saw as a dark figure stepped past it, rifle in hand, and trembled hard as the figure slowly turned to see him standing there.

The longest moment of his life passed as they stared at one another and surprise faded. Slow recognition hammered its way home as one man, then the other, said:

"Usery?"

"McGuire?"

"You bastard!"

Usery said, "Same to you!" and both guns fired as if one, booming double loud and causing the mule to shy and run to the other side of the corral, and Usery's bay, snorting loudly from seventy-five yards away, to throw its head up and whirl against the bush it was tied to, ears cocked expectantly in the direction of the noise.

But there were no more shots, and it was some while later when one man came dragging the other through the snow— in the horse's direction.

SEVEN

A TWISTING TRAIL

1

Jeremy Chance found the animal standing in front of his livery barn just before sunup next morning. It was gaunted from exertion, its legs cut and bleeding from breaking through hard-crusted snow and ice during the night, and icicles hung from its nostrils and neck where sweat had frozen as fast as it had run. Its saddle hung askew to the left, as if about to fall off, and its bridle reins were broken within a foot of the bit shanks. On the saddle, down the left side all the way to the stirrup, was blood—partly dried, partly caked and frozen, and smeared as if someone sorely wounded—or dead—had slid from the saddle.

The horse stood docilely as Jeremy came up to take hold of its bridle strap and pat it comfortingly on the neck, then to reach over and straighten the saddle. When he noticed the blood, he immediately turned and led the animal up the street to the Manor House Hotel.

"It's Quentin Usery's bay," he told Cal out in the street a few minutes later. "I'd know him anywhere."

Cal stood unshaven and bleary-eyed from the little sleep he had gotten overnight—the result of a wild night of miners' carousing in the saloons, during which the acting marshal had been forced to jail four and carry three others home through the snow. He studied the blood on the saddle with a solemn frown.

"You're certain? Absolutely certain it's Usery's?"

Jeremy nodded positively. "I must have shod that horse a dozen times, Cal. And there are no two horses alike to a blacksmith. You know that."

Cal shook his head tiredly, then looked down the street. New snow stood eighteen inches deep on the level, its surface unbroken except for the trail plowed from the livery to the hotel by Jeremy and the horse only a few minutes ago.

"Do you think we can backtrack him?" Jeremy asked, his eyes following Cal's.

Cal returned his gaze to the hostler. "I don't know. Clouds are breaking up now, but it snowed most of the night and early hours of the morning. Depends on how far he's come, on how good a trail he left, and how much a man and a saddle horse can stand in that stuff. Depends on a lot of things."

"Be pretty tough on an animal, all right," Jeremy agreed thoughtfully. "But we've got to try, don't we? We have to find out what's happened."

"Yes. I suspect we've got to try."

"Besides," Jeremy went on, trying to look hopeful, "who knows? Maybe it won't be so bad. He could have fallen off anywhere. Maybe even within sight of town."

Cal considered this with a skeptical look back at the saddle. The blood on it was no longer fresh, could even be as much as half a day old. And he knew how far a horse could travel in half a day, even through snow; he simply could not share Jeremy's hopefulness on this.

He said, "Maybe so, Jeremy. But I think we'd best plan on a little longer ride than that. Fact is, I think we should take extra horses. Ride one and lead two or three—till the first gives out, then put that one at the rear and saddle the next. Only one horse at a time breaking trail that way. You think we could scare up some extra horses around your place?"

"Sure. . . ." Then on second thought: "How many do we need? How many men do we need?"

"Well," Cal pondered, "there's not all that much a lot of men can do till we find out what's happened, and no use exciting the town any more than necessary. Right now, I'd say maybe no more than the two of us, three at the most. . . ."

"How about Clayt? Shouldn't he know? Won't he want to go with us?"

Cal had to admit he hadn't even thought of Clayt—which was what a night like he'd just had could do to a man, damned if it wasn't.

"You going to tell him?" Jeremy asked.

Cal sighed. "Yeah, I'll tell him. You go get the horses, I'll go see Clayt."

"Good enough," Jeremy said, and turned to lead the bay horse back down the street toward the livery. Cal watched him go for a second, then went wearily back inside the hotel to get his gear.

Moments later he emerged, headed in the direction of Clayton Usery's home across the arroyo at the far end of town.

2

They were doomed to failure almost from the start. Cal suspected it when the lead horse, ridden by Jeremy, slipped, broke its leg, and had to be shot not half a mile above town; he knew it when three hours and two miles farther into the Black Range the trail became so fully blanketed by new snow that it faded to nothing among the more recent game trails that crisscrossed it in every direction and left the search party hopelessly indecisive as to which way to go next.

Strangely enough, it was Clayton Usery who suggested they give up and go back. "I can't ask you men to tramp around in this snow any longer. We haven't got a snowball-in-hell's chance of finding anything without a trail to follow."

Cal, sitting twisted in his saddle a few yards ahead, nodded his own resignation. "I'm sorry, Clayt. I really am."

They were back in town by three o'clock that afternoon, cold, weary, and discouraged. Small knots of people appeared up and down the street to watch them as they rode in, their horses' hooves making squishing and sucking sounds in the now mushed-up snow and mud. Under a sky threatening to cloud back up from the north and west, they dismounted at the livery and led their animals inside, then, having cared for them, about fifteen minutes later reappeared at the door.

"You'll be reimbursed for the horse you lost, Jeremy," Clayt said. "Just bring a bill of some sort to the next committee meeting. I'll see it's taken care of."

Jeremy looked appreciative, as if he would like to simply say "Forget it" but not doing so because it was no secret that he could ill afford the gesture. No one in his business those days was rich; and a horse—especially a good horse—was no cheap loss anytime. "Thanks, Clayt."

Usery gave a little wave of the hand that implied that what he'd proposed was only right, then turned to Cal. "I have no idea what to do next, Cal. No sense going back out in the snow like this."

Cal gave him a sympathetic look. "If I had any idea where to look I'd do it anyway, Clayt. You know that, don't you?"

"Yes. I know that. Maybe when it melts off a bit, if we haven't already learned something . . . maybe then."

Cal was lost in thought a few minutes later when he stepped inside the marshal's office and found Enos Cooper hobbling in from the back room with a squinty frown on his face and an expansive air about him that said he knew something that could not go long without being told.

"Didn't find nothin', did ya?" he announced more than

asked. "Well, makes no never-mind nohow, I reckon. Good thing you're back, though. You got a visitor waitin' to see you over at the doc's. I'd scat right on over there if I was you."

Cal frowned. "Who is it? *Who* is over at the doc's?"

Enos hobbled across the room and sat down near the stove. He looked back at Cal. "You sure you ain't heard already?"

"No," Cal said patiently. "I haven't heard."

"Well, you should've," he said airily. "It's Rudabaugh. Tom Rudabaugh from Socorro."

"He's in Earl Youngblood's room," Doc Wagner told Cal only minutes later. "Rode in this morning, looking for you mostly. Said he'd spent the night at Monticello over on the Alamosa. Got caught in the storm there late yesterday, it seems. Anyway, he hustled on up here this morning, and he's been back and forth to the jail ever since, wanting to know if you've got back yet."

Cal found the two of them talking in Youngblood's room— Earl looking a good deal better than the last time he'd seen him but still not good, and Rudabaugh, whom he had met only once, looking just as he remembered him; tall, lanky, gray-haired with flowing mustache and clear eyes, and with a lean-jawed intensity that Cal had decided by now must be a singular characteristic of most western lawmen.

The sheriff rose and stuck out a knob-knuckled hand. "Good to see you again, Sawyer. Tom's been fillin' me in on the trouble you been havin'. Sorry I couldn't get here any sooner."

"Anytime's better than never," Cal said, dragging up a chair and motioning for the sheriff to retake his own. "I guess you've heard by now, too, what happened this morning?"

The lawman squinted. "You mean about Clayt Usery's brother's horse comin' in with blood on the saddle? Yeah, I heard about that. It was all over town by the time I got here. What happened? Is it another killin'?"

Cal shook his head. "I don't know. We tried backtracking the horse but lost the trail a few miles out of town. Snow had covered it over completely, and all we could tell was that the horse came down out of the Black Range sometime during the night. Without a trail to follow, well, we could have stayed up there all winter and never found where it left its rider. We never even had a chance."

"A big country, that Black Range," Rudabaugh said thoughtfully. "What would Usery be doing up there this time of year—and in this kind of weather?"

"We're not sure about that, either. No one's seen him since last Saturday night, and no one knows why he left or where he was going." Cal knew this wasn't entirely true; most people had a pretty good idea why he left—it was the where that was the question. The other just didn't seem worth going into just now.

Apparently Rudabaugh didn't think so either, for he said, "Well, one way or another, you figure one man's responsible for the killin's. A man who rides a paint mule and maybe holds a grudge against this town—is that right?"

Cal, a little surprised, glanced over at Earl Youngblood. "I'm not the only one he's talked to, Cal," that individual said hoarsely. "A lot of folks know what you think. It ain't been kept no secret, the way I get it."

Cal sighed. "Well, I don't suppose there's any reason it should be. Did anybody tell him who I think the man on the mule might be?" He looked back at Rudabaugh.

The other man nodded. "Guthrie McGuire, ain't it? Yeah, I heard that. Found it right interestin', too, if you don't mind my sayin' so. Right interestin'."

"Makes my whole theory run pretty weak, I guess—to have picked a dead man for my only suspect."

Surprisingly, the lawman did not rush to agree. "That

depends on how you look at it. You did see a man ride through here on a mule. *He* was alive, wasn't he?"

"*He*," Cal said, "without a name, also lacks a motive. And on that basis, he's nothing more than another stranger, maybe only passing through. Mysterious, suspicious, yes. But what's his motive? Why would a perfect stranger do something like this?"

"Just because you can't tag him with a motive don't mean he mightn't have one," Rudabaugh pointed out. "And you must have had a reason for coming up with McGuire for a suspect. Some way or another, you must've questioned whether or not the man was really dead."

Cal shrugged. "I read a newspaper account of his death and found it less than conclusive. At least it left room for doubt, anyway. I never claimed to have much to go on . . . just three, maybe four now, cold-blooded killings in less than two weeks. I got on to McGuire because I thought he fit a mold; he had a reason—a better one than I first thought, too, it turns out—and he'd escaped from prison only a month or so before it all happened. Trouble is, we can't find him. He strikes without being seen and leaves little or no trail. And this damn weather hasn't helped either. If it wasn't for that, we'd form posses and comb these hills till he's found. . . ." He paused, realizing he had once again fallen into the presumption that his killer had to be the stranger on the spotted mule and that that stranger had to be Guthrie McGuire. He looked at the sheriff. "Well, you see how it is. If it wasn't for this snow, I'd have every man able to sit a saddle out hunting down a dead man!"

Rudabaugh smiled. "Yes, you would, wouldn't you?" He laughed outright then and leaned back in his chair. "Well, no use me keepin' this back any longer, I reckon. As bad a bit of detective work as you may seem to have done, I for one think you've gotta be given credit for maybe—just maybe—comin' up with the right answer, anyhow. I think you've got your man pegged. What do you think of that?"

Cal could only gape at him in utter amazement. Plainly enough, Tom Rudabaugh knew something he didn't—which was pretty damned interesting, since the sheriff had been in town less than a day now and had hardly had time to do any investigating on his own. The questions were: What? How? One look over at Earl Youngblood proved that the marshal was just as surprised as Cal was. They both turned to stare expectantly back at Rudabaugh.

Again the sheriff chuckled. "It's this way, fellows—the main reason I went to the trouble to come all the way up here, along with a little business I had at Monticello. Ordinarily you folks could look into a deal like this just as well as I could. But it just happened I learned something last week that I thought you might not know and figured it might tie in. I had no idea how well, though, till I talked to you, Sawyer. No idea atall."

He paused, then smiled again. "You see, it's just like you thought: For as little reason as you had to think it, Guthrie McGuire ain't dead. He never was killed by no bear up near Las Vegas. Last Friday, it was, I got word from Santa Fe. He did escape from prison, and apparently he was seen around Las Vegas. But the man killed by the bear wasn't Guthrie McGuire. Leastways the family of one Juan José Sanchez from up Mora way don't think so. Yessir, some pore old Mexican, dressed in prison clothes and everything but not no more Guthrie McGuire than the man in the moon. He was reported missing just after the body was found, and finally had to be dug up to be identified. Had a crippled foot nobody had noticed. Juan Sanchez, no question about it. And Guthrie McGuire? Well, I put two and two together after diggin' your letter out again, Sawyer. The La Belle boys were with the posse that brought him in, and they testified against him in court. And I reckon he's just the kind to remember that. I led the posse and sat through the trial, so I oughta know. Sure, none of this is proof any more than what you had before. But I say it's somethin' to go on, and if hunches ever were worth anything to a lawman—and I believe strongly that they always have been—then my hunch that you've pegged your man ain't a bad one. All you gotta do is find him."

Cal wagged his head, still in amazement. "But how did they explain McGuire's clothing and personal effects found on the body? And couldn't they tell from the first that the dead man was a Mexican? Certainly McGuire was no Mexican."

The sheriff looked as if he had anticipated this question. "Well, I reckon this may be conjecture, but it seems pretty probable that McGuire actually rigged the whole thing. Either found pore old Juan José already dead, or killed him himself and made it look like a bear done it. Folks around Santa Fe and Las Vegas both figure McGuire wanted to have himself declared dead, mostly so he could make his getaway clean and not have wanted posters houndin' him forever. As far as the dead man bein' a Mexican . . . well, McGuire's a dark-complected man himself. Could almost pass for a Mexican. That part's the easiest of all to explain."

Once again Cal wagged his head. "So our killer may be McGuire after all—and all I've got to do now is find him!" He looked at Rudabaugh expectantly. "Sheriff, what do you plan to do? Will you stay to help us?"

The lawman shook his head. "I'm sorry, boy. I've got to get back. We've got problems down Socorro way, too, and I'm short-handed for help right now. You'll have to take care of it yourselves—which I'm sure you can do, now that you know almost for sure who you're after."

"You're sure you won't reconsider?"

Again a shake of the head. "I'm already a day overdue getting back," he said. "I'm sorry, son. I really am. But there's actually nothin' I can do that you can't. Soon as this snow is melted some, get some men and go after him. And watch the town; don't let folks go crazy with fear and go shootin' at each other. That's all I can tell you . . . all I could do if I stayed here."

Cal could see it was no use. He sighed. "Well, thanks for bringing us word of McGuire, Sheriff. When will you be going back?"

"In the mornin', son," Rudabaugh said. "First thing tomorrow mornin', weather permittin', o' course."

3

It did not snow again that night. To almost everyone's surprise, the storm clouds forming to the north and west somehow passed on by and left the morning to dawn cold and very, very clear. Cal watched Sheriff Rudabaugh ride out at eight, then went over to the jail and released the four miners he had jailed for drunkenness two nights before. From there, he breakfasted at the Manor House, then walked to the livery and saddled his grulla. In his present mood of deep frustration and discouragement, he'd decided that a trip out to the homestead might help his frame of mind. And he did need to check up on things there.

On his way out of town, he stopped by the Usery home and called for Clayt.

"He could have stayed," he told the other man after relating the news Rudabaugh had delivered. "He could have stayed to help."

There was an inexplicably worried look on Usery's face as he replied, "Maybe. But you're probably lucky he came at all. And with this snow on the ground, he'd probably have only cooled his heels waiting around to be able to do something. I'm afraid it's still our baby, Cal."

"Yeah," Cal said. "Our baby."

They talked a few moments more, mostly about what the sheriff had said about Guthrie McGuire, and decided that for the moment it was information best kept under their hats. An already nervous town did not need anything new to excite it. For now, there was not much more they could do about it. The same was true of their desire to find out what had happened to Quentin. Cal could only admire Clayt for his determination—despite probable criticism—not to go rushing out against all odds in search of his brother. A weaker man would have, he knew.

"Well," Cal told him finally, "I'm going to make a run out to my place, see if I have any cows still alive. Maybe in a day or two things will be such we can go out looking for Quentin again. Maybe we'll find something this time."

"I hope so," Usery said solemnly. "I hope so."

Outside of town, Cal quickly found the going easiest whenever he could stick to the ridgetops. The snow was windswept and much less deep there, and if not truly easy it was at least possible for the horse to make the trip without suffering complete exhaustion lunging from drift to drift along the canyon bottoms.

Even so, the conditions added half an hour to the short trip, and Cal was forced to rest the horse when he got there. At the corrals he found over half his cows and one bull standing, bawling, and reluctantly he opened the gate to one of the two small grama grass haystacks nearby. Then he went inside the cabin, found a tin of coffee and a pot, filled this with clean snow, and soon had water boiling on the stove. He took a noon meal of cold beef jerky, canned fruit, and coffee, cleaned up about the house, and then went back outside.

The cows and the lone bull were not only still working on the haystack but also had better than half demolished it by now. Presently he decided they'd had enough and waded across to the haystack to shoo them out. No sooner had he done this than he realized that left alone they would do nothing more than hang around waiting to be fed again, and might even break down the fence. A mistake in the first place to have let them inside, he knew now that before

going back to town he would have to haze them back toward the brushy canyons to the west, where browse was
ample and maybe they would stay.

He busied himself for about an hour fixing a place in the
haystack fence where the bull had leaned on a post and had
indeed already broken the fence, then checked around to
see if there was anything else that needed tending to.
Satisfied that there was not, he decided it was not too soon
to be heading back to town.

Finding the grulla well rested now, he mounted up and
shortly had the small herd of cattle moving out in a westerly
direction. They went easily—which was fortunate, for in the
snow he could never have handled them if they had tried to
break or scatter—and after about half a mile he figured he
had pushed them far enough. He stopped and watched as
they meandered into the trees, then reined the horse back in
the direction of town.

He topped the first long ridge; then, as he had done that
morning, he began angling down it. He rode leisurely, letting the horse pick the easiest going, and feeling for the first
time during the day a comfortable measure of warmth from
the sun.

He wasn't sure when he first noticed the movement on the
ridge opposite him; it was about two hundred yards away,
across the canyon, and at first he thought it only a jay flit-
ting from one tree to the other. But then he seemed to sense
it more than see it—even when he looked away. It was as if
it were following him, keeping pace among the dense junipers that capped the other ridge. A short way farther and
he knew he caught a movement out the corner of his eye.
He stopped and turned in the saddle. It had come from just
slightly behind him.

For almost a minute he sat there, perfectly still except for
the slow pattern movement of his eyes scanning the ridge.
All he saw were trees and snow. Nothing moved. He relaxed

only slightly, but after a few seconds more shrugged uneasily and turned again in the saddle.

It was then, as he turned, that he caught the flash in the trees; a glint like that of sunlight off of metal or glass. A sudden intuition stirred within him, told him to dive for safety. But in the same instant that he bunched his muscles for the dive, a loud crack sounded and almost simultaneously he felt a blow to his head and his hat flew off. He felt himself being half propelled, half slipping from the saddle, the horse shying as he did and stepping sharply sideways, dumping him like a sack of meal in the snow.

Somehow the sudden cold was renewed shock enough that he did not immediately pass out. But he felt numb, paralyzed down his right side, and it was all he could do to move; there was a survival instinct, not strong there on the verge of unconsciousness, but there nevertheless. Slowly, painfully, he rolled onto his stomach, and despite the fact that it seemed like a dead weight on the end of his neck, he managed to raise his head.

At first all was hazy in front of him, and his head swam. He knew he was going to black out at any moment. He closed his eyes, trying to rest them in what would have seemed to an onlooker nothing more than a slow blinking movement. Upon reopening them, he was vaguely surprised to see the far ridge come briefly into focus, and somehow he did not count it a dream what he saw skylined on the horizon in his last conscious moment.

Sitting there, arrogantly posed in bold contrast to all that was around him now, was the rider on the spotted mule.

EIGHT

SIDELINED

1

Cal awoke to pain and darkness and what had to be at least
semidelirium. He was both hot and cold, sweating amid se-
vere chills, and could not help feeling like a being detached
from its own body. He did not know where he was or how
he got there. He couldn't even remember what had happened to him. He knew only that his head hurt terribly and
that dizziness and nausea swept him every time he tried to
move. He suspected that someone else was near him, but he
was in no condition to tell for sure, or determine who. Finally he lay very still, and after a while he fell once again
into a fitful sleep.

The next time he awoke it was to no less pain, but no
longer to the delirium or chills. There was a faint light in the
room now, and he knew, too, that he was in the softest bed
he'd known since his boyhood; that the room held the light,
strange smell of perfume mixed with something like wood-
smoke; and that it was very warm. Somehow he reasoned
that this must be a woman's bedroom . . . and that it had a
stove in it somewhere, for it certainly would not have been
so warm otherwise. Slowly memory began to return, but still
he could not figure out where he was or how he'd gotten
there.

He slept again, dozing, dreaming erratically of things that
made little sense and that could not be connected one to the

other, and when he awoke the next time it was to full daylight and cool, soft hands and a damp cloth caressing his
forehead. It was a moment before the hazy image behind
the hands became a face—a pretty, feminine face—and
finally came clear enough that he thought he knew whose it
was.

"Jenny? Is it you?"

"Yes," she said softly. Then a worried frown creased her
forehead. "Why? Can't you see me?"

"You . . . look a little fuzzy," he managed. His voice was
weak and thick, and he wanted to clear it, but the pain in
his head dissuaded him from even this much effort. For the
first time consciously, he raised a hand to his head and
found it heavily bandaged.

"You've a gunshot wound, Cal. A half-inch gash right
across the top of your head. I know it hurts, but you were
really very lucky. A smidgeon lower and the doc says you
wouldn't have lasted three seconds."

He nodded more with his eyes than with his head. "Good
thing for a thick skull, huh?"

She smiled weakly and continued to bathe his face and
forehead beneath the bandage with the cloth. "Do you want
anything? A drink of water? Something to eat?"

There was a barely perceptible wag of the head. "Maybe
later."

"Your face is still hot. Do you feel sick?"

"A little. Mostly I hurt, though."

"Your head, I know . . ."

But he said, "My right shoulder, too. And my arm—I almost can't raise it."

She seemed a little surprised at this. "I didn't know about
that. You must have hurt it when you fell. Do you remember
anything of that? How you were shot?"

Cal closed his eyes for a second. Did he remember! The
scene was so vivid in his mind he could almost hear the shot
echoing down the canyon and feel the cold snow against his

face, see clearly the rider facing him, sentinel-like, from the opposite ridge. "He shot me from ambush, Jenny. I never saw him till I was down."

"You saw him?"

His nod was again very slight. "The man on the mule," he said. "I saw him clearly."

Somehow she did not look surprised. "We suspected as much, but we had no way of knowing for sure," she said. "The men who found you heard the shot, but by the time they got to you there was no one else to be seen, and you were unconscious." She paused. "You were lucky there, too, Cal. If they hadn't heard that shot and rode toward it, you might very well have lain there and bled or frozen to death."

"Who was it that found me?" he asked, instantly curious. "And where am I? What day is it?"

"You're at Uncle Caleb's, and you were brought in just before sundown yesterday by two of Clayt Usery's cowboys, who were on their way into town from the Triple U when they found you. They brought you straight to Doc Wagner's, who then had you brought straight here because he wanted someone to stay with you constantly until your fever passed. I volunteered for the job, and haven't left you for more than a few minutes at a time since."

Cal pursed his lips, marveling. "Only yesterday? I feel like I've been out for days."

"Well," Jenny said, "for all practical purposes you still will be. Doc says you're to stay right where you are for at least another couple of days, and no telling even then when you'll really be up and around."

He grimaced at this. "I'd hoped to form a posse to go after McGuire again by now," he said, disappointment etched on his face. "And Quentin Usery—has there been any news of him? I promised Clayt. . . ."

She looked at him sympathetically. "I'm afraid that's out of the question, Cal. Quentin still hasn't been found, but I doubt if you could walk across this room by yourself, much less lead a posse anywhere. Besides, what makes you think you're the only one who can handle that bit of business, anyway?"

He stared at her. "What do you mean?"

"I mean, Cal, it's something that some folks decided couldn't wait any longer. Even with the snow . . . something had to be done."

Still he stared at her, some but possibly not all of what she implied coming clear.

"Cal," she went on, "a man, besides yourself, was shot at yesterday. An innocent cowhand riding a paint horse. A couple of miners saw him top a ridge and started shooting before anyone realized what was going on. It was pure luck the man wasn't killed." She gave him a meaningful look. "Guthrie McGuire, if that's who the killer is, has got to be found and stopped before this town goes berserk. It's something that couldn't wait any longer."

"Meaning a posse has already gone out," Cal concluded, surprised but not astonished.

"Yes. This morning, first thing."

"Who's leading them?"

"Clayt Usery, Jeremy Chance, Bay Calhoun, Lige Martin. About a dozen men went with them. Mostly cowhands from Usery's Triple U or Martin's Bar M, but a couple of miners, too. Clayt told us about what Tom Rudabaugh said about McGuire's not being dead. They are looking both for him and Quentin Usery, and they claimed they weren't coming back till they found one or both."

Cal considered this for a moment, accepted it, and finally said, "Well, I hope no more cowhands on paint horses come riding over the hill while they're about it. Who's watching the town? Are the mines open again? Has there been any trouble?"

She shrugged. "Not much trouble, I guess, although I can't really say anybody's watching anything officially. The Glory Be and the Silver Brick reopened today, and the mill will be running on a part-time basis tomorrow. I think Usery was almost forced into it, snow or no snow. Things were just getting too tense around town. There were fights in at least two saloons last night, and a couple of men almost came to a shootout in an argument over who ought to be doing what about the killings."

"Tom Rudabaugh warned against that," Cal said fatalistically. "I don't figure anyone ought to be surprised."

"Then you understand why the posse went out without you?"

He looked rather dismally down at himself and said, "Not much choice they had, was there?"

She didn't say anything, and after a moment he let his eyes roam about the room, cataloguing its features as he went: window curtains that were crisp, pretty, and frilled; a dresser and mirror along one wall, complete with ladies' toiletries, brushes, and combs; a wardrobe closet a few feet away, closed at the moment but just the type to contain a lady's finery; and out from one corner, a luxury of luxuries among bedrooms to be found around Grafton, a small pot-belly stove, which would keep the room warm on even the most wintry of nights. Beside the bed was a hide-covered rocker, in which he figured Jenny must have spent most, if not all, of the night.

"It's your room, isn't it? Your bed even."

"Yes," she replied with a little smile. "Do you mean to tell me you only now figured that out?"

"Just one of the penalties for being thick-skulled," he said, and was then struck with another belated revelation. He looked down at himself, then at the sleeve of his half-raised left arm. It barely extended beyond his elbow. "Whose pajamas are these?"

Jenny laughed. "Uncle Caleb's. And if you think that's funny, you should see the legs. You have very knobby shins, Cal."

He stared at her intently. "Who . . . put these on me?"

She gave him a coy grin, coupled with a suggestive flash of the eye that made it impossible for him not to catch the implication. "Well, someone had to do it," she protested. "And I *am* your nurse. . . ."

"Jenny . . ." he said, trying to rise. "If you . . ." But he didn't finish; the moment he raised his head from the pillow things began to spin and the nausea struck once more. He collapsed back, his face pale and his head thundering with pain.

"Now you've done it!" Jenny said, bending over him and once again bathing his face with the damp cloth. "I'm sorry, Cal. I shouldn't have teased you. You're not ready to be moving around yet, and I've let you talk too long. Just lie still and rest. . . . Are you better now?"

"Yeah," he lied. "I was just a little dizzy, I guess."

She studied him skeptically. "Well, just to make sure, I'm going to leave you for a while—see if you'll go back to sleep. You will stay still, won't you?"

Cal smiled very weakly. There was hardly any question about that. He lay there for several minutes after she was gone, waiting for the pain and nausea to subside and dazedly marveling at how little effort had been required to bring either sensation on.

Finally, feeling somewhat better at last, he drifted into a relatively quiet sleep.

2

Cal woke up the next time shortly before noon, his fever gone and feeling hungry. Jenny brought him a bowl of hot broth and a cup of weak tea to go with it. He downed both while grumping something to the effect that it was a fine thing when a man couldn't get any solid food to eat, only to find in the end that it was really all he wanted and all he could hold, anyway.

He passed the afternoon restlessly in bed, Jenny coming and going but never staying for long at a time, and by evening he was able to sit propped against his upright pillow without becoming dizzy or nauseous. When Doc Wagner came by to see him, he even argued he was able now to leave the room in lieu of having to use a bedpan, but the doc would have none of that.

"You get out of that bed by yourself before tomorrow," he said sternly, "and you'll get no sympathy from me when you fall and crack your head for good. You lost a lot of blood, young man. Be a day or so before you've the strength to sit up in the outhouse alone, much less do anything else. You do as I say, you hear?"

"It's just that bedpans are so damned demeaning," Cal complained miserably.

The doc grinned at him. "Be all right if it wasn't a pretty young thing like Jenny having to carry it in and out for you, though, wouldn't it?" He paused, working with a new bandage, then went on, "But don't you go fooling yourself none, boy; that gal ain't no naïve little hand-twister like a lot of these around here. No, sir! Make a damn good nurse full-time, she would. Good wife, too, if you get what I mean."

Cal got it, but he had no intention of following up on it. He changed the subject, albeit abruptly, and despite the doc's impish wink. "Any news of the posse yet?"

"Nary hide nor hair," the other man said as he finished with the bandages and began closing up his bag. "And don't you fret about 'em, either. Whatever they're doing out there, ain't no way you could be of any help to 'em. That's the cinch of the year." He stood at the door. "You call for me if you need anything, you hear?"

Cal watched him go with the feeling that nothing he'd ever asked before had been so completely evaded. Which only left him more starved than ever for news of what was going on. Unfortunately, he learned no more from Jenny later that evening, or Cora Usery, who stopped by briefly after supper, or Aunt Martha and Caleb, who ducked in just before bedtime.

He slept poorly that night, maybe because he had slept so much during the day, but, too, at least in part because of things on his mind. Things he could not dismiss. An almost obsessive concern with the man on the spotted mule; the man who had shot him and others, who threatened in a deeply sinister way to go on shooting until he was either stopped or there was nobody left to shoot. A kind of vengeance commanded by a hatred so apparently deep that it might even become insatiable. Controlled, methodical, insatiable. Something Cal could scarcely even fathom.

Oh sure, Celsa's story in mind, and if the killer was indeed Guthrie McGuire, he could understand it up to a point—and that point was the one at which Cal himself had become the target! Until then it had made whatever perverse sense these kinds of things make, for at least the others who had been shot had been citizens of Grafton at the time of McGuire's trouble; they were all known to him. Whether victims because of specific personal grievances or random targets picked from the whole, not one of them was a perfect stranger. McGuire must have known each quite well, in fact. The La Belles, Little Mike, Quentin Usery . . . all of them. But not Cal Sawyer. . . .

So why? *Why me?* Mistaken identity or random selection at its purest. He wondered . . . and became more, rather than less, skeptical. He believed strongly—had when it happened and did now—that he had been very carefully stalked by his attacker, maybe for even longer than he had realized. Which would lead one to believe that none of it was by accident or chance; that he may have been a target selected more carefully than not. And why would Guthrie McGuire, a man he had never met, do that?

The question lingered, but he could find no satisfactory answer for it.

The next day passed with Cal making reasonable progress toward recovery, but with no word at all from or about the posse. Jenny came by at regular intervals, but did not stay with him constantly, as she had done most of the day before. So, bored silly, by afternoon he was at least able to negotiate the open distance between the bed and the window, where he sat for almost an hour simply watching what little went on outside.

That it was a side window that did not look directly onto Main Street—except at a very narrow angle aimed at a vacant lot between the jail and Calhoun's funeral parlor—bothered him not in the least. He was able to obtain frequent though brief glimpses of the traffic on the street, and it was of distinct interest to him to be able to observe how much snow remained as a result of the last storm. Of this he had a good view, and certainly there was more than he had hoped, for the days had apparently remained quite cold. But there were a few open hillsides north of town where patches of ground showed through, and this was usually a sign that rapid melting was beginning to occur. Main Street, on the other hand, was still a quagmire, and Cal could imagine what it was like in the mountains to the west where the snow would be, from the start, much deeper and slower to melt. He did not envy that posse out there even a little bit.

He slept better that night and felt better yet the following day. But that didn't mean he was any more satisfied with his situation. The doc still wouldn't let him leave the house; there was yet no news of the posse; and worst of all, Jenny had to spend most of the day at the *Myriad* cleaning type used in one day's paper and helping Caleb get things in order for the next. Thus he was alone most of the time, which added to his boredom, he figured, fourfold and more.

That night, however, he was at least able to take supper at the family dining table instead of in his room, and afterward he and Caleb sat in the parlor, smoking and talking, while the women did the dishes. Caleb even offered him a glass of brandy, and Jenny came later to curl up before the fireplace and listen to the men talk. She would have nothing to do, however, with Cal staying up late, and promptly at nine o'clock shoved him off to his room to go to bed.

"If you'll be good and get a good night's sleep," she told him, "I'll even let you take me to church tomorrow."

"Oh you will, will you?" he said a bit archly. Then he realized that he hadn't even known it would be Sunday. Three days had passed already since he had been shot. Three days! "What about the doc? What'll he say?"

"Don't you worry about him," Jenny said. "I've already talked to him. He only said to take it easy; otherwise, okay. You're coming along even faster than he figured you would."

"That old devil," Cal muttered. "Told me this morning it would be at least two more days before I could leave the house!"

He didn't know what time it was later on when he had the nightmare. He had gone to sleep easily enough, more so than usual even. And it wasn't the first time it had happened. At least twice before, in the past few nights, he'd had the same dream; but never so vividly, never right down to the heart-pounding and the pain like this. Cal against the rider on the mule; he disarmed and the rider bearing down with rifle in one hand, pistol in the other, and a tremendous Bowie knife clenched between his teeth . . . out in the open with nowhere to go, the rider coming faster, faster. Always before it had ended with Cal waking up in a sweat before the rider reached him or fired off a shot. But this time the other man kept coming, closer and closer, the mule's hooves pounding flat and loud against hard, dry ground, coming close enough that for the first time Cal could clearly see the rider's face—which he fully expected to be that of Guthrie McGuire.

But there was no face! It was not, could not be McGuire. He rode right down on Cal, thundered past . . . and there was no face. No eyes, no features, no face—not that of the man Cal had seen ride through town that day or any other. He was indeed a ghost! *A ghost on a spotted mule!* Cal whirled to watch him ride off and disappear, but instead, the ghost hauled the mule around and came again, this time rifle and pistol alike belching flame and smoke as if they were cannon on the goriest battlefields of the Great War.

Then came the pain, in his head and down his right shoulder and into his arm. And then he was awake, sitting on the edge of his bed, the covers flung clear and his heart pounding a hundred times a minute. Sweat had popped out on his forehead, his mouth was very, very dry, and his breathing came in great gulps.

It was then that the door to his room swung open and someone stood there, lamp in hand, calling his name. It was Jenny, dressed in a soft cotton peignoir that the lamplight all but shone through, her blond hair billowing down her back and framing her face so that her high cheekbones were softened and her eyes were widened even more than the occasion demanded. Her breasts stood full and high against the peignoir, but the outline of the rest of her body was just traceable within the garment's loose confines.

"Cal! Are you all right?" She had already closed the door, presumably to keep from disturbing the rest of the house. She sat the lamp, turned low, on something nearby and came toward him. "You called out. I was afraid something had happened."

"I'm . . . all right," he said hoarsely. "It was just a nightmare."

She studied him skeptically. "You woke me up. I was afraid Uncle Caleb and Aunt Martha would hear you too, although I don't think they did. . . . Lordy, it took me forever just to get this lamp lit!" Cal knew she slept on a sofa in the parlor not more than twenty feet from his door; Caleb and Martha's room, on the other hand, was on the opposite side of the house.

"Why, you're soaking wet, Cal," Jenny said, reaching out

to touch his nightshirt at the chest. "We may have to get Uncle's pajamas back out for you, after all."

Suddenly he felt quite embarrassed. He had no use for nightshirts; never had. They were too much like dresses; they left his legs bare, and they rolled up under him every time he turned. A man could sleep in his underwear, or nothing, a hell of a lot better. But Jenny had brought it to him, had insisted . . . and right now the damned thing was up over his knees in such a fashion that he thought he knew how ladies must feel in similar situations. He tugged at it impatiently, and Jenny laughed.

"Oh Cal—you don't have to hide your knees. You know I've seen them already."

He glared at her. "Not while I was awake and could do something about it, you didn't!"

She laughed again. "My, what modesty! I never would have thought it of you, Cal."

"You've never shown me your knees," he grumbled back.

She stepped back a couple of steps, a curious look on her face. "I don't remember ever knowing you wanted to look," she said, despite a sudden self-conciousness about things that caused her to clutch the front of her peignoir as if unsure it had not been open and just then realizing how she herself was dressed.

And the light was behind her now, creating a silhouette of her body through the gown and whatever she had on underneath. One look at Cal's mesmerized expression told her this, and she stepped quickly to the side, where the effect was immediately broken. Jenny was no prude, but the incident brought a mighty blush to her face just the same.

Cal smiled broadly. "We're even," he said.

"And you're horrid!" she shot back, although a bit weakly. "You stared, Cal Sawyer! You really stared!"

"I apologize," he said, still smiling. "But like I said, we're even. I think I owed you that—or you owed me. I'm not sure which."

Jenny had a very dismal look on her face then. "I didn't really *see* you, Cal," she admitted. "I was only teasing—Uncle Caleb and the doc put those pajamas on you. I wasn't even in the room."

"Well, *that's* a relief!"

She eyed him skeptically, then resignedly, and as she recovered her composure, even a bit defiantly. "Well, you're not going back to bed in that nightshirt. You'll have to change." Carefully avoiding the lamp this time, she walked over to the dresser and took out her uncle's pajamas, left there just in case. She tossed them over to Cal.

He caught them, but made no move to do anything with them. Rather, he looked at Jenny, who so far simply stayed where she was, as if waiting vaguely for some reaction from him. She hardly seemed to realize he would have to take one thing off to put the other on.

"Well," he said at last, "are you going to just stand there —or are you going to help?"

To her credit, a tiny gulp and but the slightest crimson rise to her face represented her only outward loss of composure. "Neither," she said in a low voice, adding, "Just you set that lamp outside when you're through."

And then she fled the room.

3

The Reverend Nathan Gregg occupied the pulpit of the Grafton Methodist Church looking much like a fiery-eyed disciple of the very devil he so regularly spoke out against. A meek-looking man anywhere else, before his congregation he grew into a powerful force, a speaker of no small magnitude whose voice rang throughout his tiny, rough-hewn sanctuary from crevice to crack with an authority that never failed to settle a hush over even the most restless of children. But it wasn't all thundering hell's fire and brimstone;

he could plead, cajole, and soothe as well as any man. He did not hold his audience, he captivated them. And he had a full church every Sunday, a fact of which he was understandably proud and of which (mortal man that he was) he did not hesitate to remind the church elders at each and every opportunity.

Today was no real exception. Even Cal sat half enthralled by the reverend's oratory, despite the fact that he was still lightheaded from the short walk up the street and across the bridge to the church, and even more so despite the very heady sensation of sitting jammed next to Jenny in a pew so tightly packed that their shoulders and thighs touched unavoidably and he could actually feel the slight rise and fall of her with each and every breath she took.

Her very presence was distraction enough. She wore a dark skirt with white bodice and tight waist that made her seem not only taller but also more slender and fuller of bosom; a dark, broad-billed Sunday hat with a light mesh veil hanging down just enough to cover her eyes; and she smelled pleasantly of faint jasmine, clean and fresh and alluring, to the point that Cal actually felt a giddy sense of torture just sitting next to her. It was such a feeling that he was both relieved and disappointed at the same time when the final hymn was sung and the congregation dismissed a few minutes later.

At the door he shook hands with Rev. Gregg. "That was a fine sermon, Reverend."

The minister smiled blandly, and added an appropriately grateful nod. "Thank you, my boy," he said. "Very kind of you to say that. Good to see you up and about again, too. How's the wound?"

Cal continued to wear the bandage on his head—mostly now to hide the spot where the doc had shaved his hair—and the chagrin at having to be seen one way was outweighed only by what would have been had the other been the case. "Healing," he said. "Healing just fine."

"Glad to hear that, my son," Rev. Gregg said. "Such a terrible thing, this shooting and killing. Terrible, terrible thing." He shook his head sadly.

Outside it was clear, but a cold wind whipped, and despite heavy coats and hats few were lingering to visit. One or two came over to ask Cal how he was doing and to express regret at what had happened to him, and banker Mel Cole stopped to voice his concern that no word had yet been heard from the posse.

"It's got me bothered, too," Cal told him. "But I don't know what we can do other than to wait. They've got to come back in soon. Supplies will run low, if nothing else."

"Do you think they have a chance of finding our man, or Quentin Usery, either one?" the banker asked seriously.

"I hope so," Cal said. "I sure as hell hope so."

It was an hour later, as they sat down for Sunday dinner—and sooner than Cal expected—that they found out. Aunt Martha had just served a huge platter of fried chicken, coupled with gravy, potatoes, fresh bread, honey, and butter, when a knock at the front door interrupted them. Caleb left to answer it, then almost immediately called for Cal. Standing inside the door was Bay Calhoun's oldest son.

"My ma . . . told me to come . . . t-tell you," he said, shivering from the cold made worse by the fact that he had apparently left home so excited he had forgotten his coat. "The p-posse's comin'. I—I seen 'em m-myself, comin' down the Victorio road."

Cal and Caleb both went for their coats, and were out in the street a few moments later when the first small cluster of riders and pack animals rounded the corner just beyond the Pioneer Saloon. Among them were Clayton Usery and Jeremy Chance. Cal and Caleb met them in front of the livery.

"Well," Cal asked, "did you find anything?" He couldn't tell whether the expression on Usery's face was one of discouragement or fatigue or both. But rather plainly it was not one to be expected from a man who had just enjoyed a completely successful mission.

The older man swung down and handed his reins to Jeremy. "We found something," he said dourly. He pointed back up the street where three more riders had just dismounted in front of Bay Calhoun's undertaking establishment. They were removing a tarp from something strapped to the back of one of the pack horses.

"A body," Cal said; then, almost afraid to ask but compelled to anyway: "How? Where? Who is it?" __

Usery acknowledged the questions but did not rush to answer them all in one breath the way they had been asked. "Yesterday, before noon, we found what we knew to have been an abandoned prospector's cabin. It's about ten miles from here, and was one of the last places we'd thought to look. There was no one there at the time, but it didn't take much to see that the house had been lived in, possibly for several days or even weeks, and recently. Out back we found where an animal had been kept in the corral—"

"A mule?" Cal put in, excitedly. "Could it have been a mule?"

Uscry nodded. "Jeremy, here, said he'd swear to it. Said he'd almost swear the tracks were the same as he'd seen outside Mike Wonderly's house, day after Mike was killed." Cal looked at Jeremy, who nodded his confirmation, then back at Usery. The latter's eyes were very tired as they met Cal's. "Our man's hideout, Cal. No doubt about it."

"But where was he? He wasn't there?"

"We thought not, at first. But then a couple of the men got to looking around a ways from the cabin, and they found that"—he pointed toward the tarp-covered form now being carried inside the funeral parlor—"half buried in a snowbank."

Cal's gaze traveled from the scene up the street back to Usery. "Who is it, Clayt? For God's sake, tell us who it is!"

There was more than a tinge of exasperation and misery

in the other man's eyes as he answered, "We don't know, Cal. That's the trouble—we just plain damn can't tell!"

"*You can't tell?*"

"You'll have to see the body, boy. Evidently someone had tried to bury it—we found mud and rocks in the clothing as if it had been covered over—but whoever it was didn't do much of a job. Varmints—probably coyotes—dug it up. Chewed hell out of it . . . face gone, one arm mangled, stomach ripped open . . ." He wagged his head soberly. "Beyond that all we could tell for sure was that it was a man, and that he had been shot, which is probably what killed him. Dead center in the chest, it was, and Bay figured him dead several days, maybe even a week. We think maybe it's Guthrie McGuire, but there just isn't enough left to recognize."

Cal had a very strange look on his face and an even stranger feeling in his gut. "Clayt, you're certain it isn't Quentin? There was nothing you, his own brother, couldn't identify?"

"What was left of his clothes were not Quentin's," Usery said, as if he had indeed considered the possibility in some depth already. "He was about the right size and build, dark hair . . . but there was so much of him gone. . . ." His voice cracked with real agony and his words were choked off. It was plain that he, as well as Cal, had recalled how once already Guthrie McGuire had been taken for dead under all too similar a set of circumstances.

Cal looked at him sympathetically but evenly, and also around at Jeremy and Caleb. "Somebody correct me if I'm wrong," he said, "but weren't McGuire and Quentin about the same size and build? Both dark-complected—black hair, dark eyes? I know the man I saw ride through here on the spotted mule was like that. Badly mutilated, might one not be mistaken for the other? And if someone killed McGuire, why wouldn't he, or they, come in and report it?"

The three men looked at him in studied, somber silence.

Finally Usery said, "I think you better come have a look at the body, Cal. It's not a pretty sight, but maybe you'd at least recognize the clothes."

Jeremy, saying he'd seen enough already, led the horses on inside the livery, while Cal and Caleb went with Usery over to the funeral parlor.

Inside, Cal took one look at the body, allowed that it could have been the same clothing the man on the mule had worn the day Cal saw him ride through town, then went out back and threw up.

NINE

THE ROAD TO BITTER TRUTH

1

The next day or so was as uneasy a time as ever around Grafton. The body brought in by the posse simply could not be identified, thus represented only another dead man, possibly one more murder, and no relief at all from the menace that had threatened the town for almost two weeks. Cal Sawyer had said that yes, the dead man's clothing, ripped and torn though it was, could have been that worn by the man on the mule, who was thought to be Guthrie McGuire, who in turn was thought to be the killer. But even if Cal had been certain, the story of McGuire's supposed death up near Las Vegas had been generally exposed for what it was now; an event fraught not only with false assumptions from the beginning, but apparently a carefully calculated piece of deceit on McGuire's part to boot. And what manner of similar circumstances might people be expected to believe twice? Another badly mangled body, unrecognizable, with clothing that could be so easily switched? It seemed too much of a coincidence for even the most gullible to fall for a second time. Too much even for Clayton Usery, who wanted so very much to believe that the dead man was somehow McGuire and not his own brother Quentin. Too much even for him.

Too, there also existed the very troublesome matter of the probable time of death. On Saturday, the day the body was found, Bay Calhoun had said five days to a week, no more and probably no less, since death had occurred. Saturday counted back five days came to at least Tuesday. Assuming no serious miscalculation in this respect, and that the dead man really was Guthrie McGuire, then who was the rider on the spotted mule who took a shot at Cal on Wednesday? And what day had Quentin Usery's horse shown up in town with blood on its saddle—Tuesday morning? Of course. And was it logical to read McGuire's death into any of this? Not many thought so.

But no man's death can be officially declared on speculation alone. The sad, undeniable fact remained: The body had been rendered utterly unrecognizable. And worse, by Monday, despite the fact that it had gone several days frozen or near frozen before being found, its condition was such that burial could no longer be postponed. Bay Calhoun called it the beginning of advanced decomposition; everyone else called it, more crudely but equally graphic in description, plain, flat ripe.

Thus, early that afternoon, the man was laid to rest in the Grafton cemetery, an unmarked cross at the head of the grave and with but half a dozen persons present to observe the ceremony. Rev. Nathan Gregg dutifully mumbled a few words of Scripture; Bay Calhoun, Cal, and Clayt Usery stood by as witnesses; and two others, hired out of the saloon to dig the grave, covered it back over when the others were through. A short while later Celsa Jaramillo came by to kneel at the grave of her friend, Cassie McGuire, and then to pause curiously, thoughtfully, before the fresh mound of dirt left by the burial crew. But then she, too, was gone with more pressing matters on her mind, and for now at least it was as if the man had never lived.

That night, even though he had moved back to his room at the hotel now, Cal took supper at the Caleb Harvey house. Afterward, he and Caleb retired to the parlor and were a little while later joined by Jenny and Aunt Martha.

They talked for a while; then, after a bit, Aunt Martha excused herself to go to bed. A few minutes later Caleb was about to do the same, and Cal was contemplating saying good night himself when a knock at the front door startled them.

Caleb went to answer the knock and was even more startled to find Clayt and Cora Usery standing there.

"Sorry to bother you so late, Caleb," Usery told him, hat in hand. "I need to talk to Cal, and old Enos over at the jail told us he might still be here."

"Of course," Caleb said. "He's inside. Here, let me take your coats."

"Hello, Jenny. Cal," Usery said as he and Cora took seats on the sofa. It was Cora, however, who looked uneasily around as Caleb came into the room after putting up their coats. "Where is Martha?" she asked. "Are we keeping you up, Caleb? I know Cal looked as if he was about to leave when we came in."

Caleb gave her a reassuring look. "Martha's gone to bed, but you wouldn't have come here at all if it wasn't something important. Don't worry yourself on my account."

"Mine either," Cal put in. "What's the problem, Clayt?"

Usery looked at him with something of a sigh. "Well, first of all: Did you know that Earl Youngblood is leaving town tomorrow?"

Cal frowned. He hadn't seen Earl since the day Tom Rudabaugh was in town. "No—I didn't know that. Where is he going? Why?"

"He's headed back East—St. Louis, I think. Says he's through marshaling. Says the doc tells him he's messed up worse inside than was first thought, that he needs better care than he can get here. He has a brother in St. Louis, and Doc tells him there are good doctors there."

"I had no idea he was even up to a trip like that yet."

"He may not be. Only thing is, Doc says he's not likely to get any better without the right kind of care. I guess under those circumstances he figures the sooner the better, that it might get too late altogether if he waits much longer."

"When did you learn this, Clayt?" Caleb asked.

"This afternoon, since the burial. And it causes a problem right now because the deal we made with Cal was for him to fill in as marshal till Earl got well enough to come back on the job—which of course isn't ever going to happen now." He looked back at Cal. "I've talked with Jeremy and Bay about it, Cal. We've got to have a marshal, and we just can't get anybody else on so short a notice. We're asking if you'll stay on at least until this killing business is cleared up. I know you've still got that wound on your head, but . . ."

Cal wagged his head in somewhat resigned fatalism. "I'm tempted to use that as an excuse; I really am. But Doc says I'm all right, that it's just a matter of healing now. And I guess I knew all along that Earl might never retake the job. I just hadn't thought of him leaving like this. . . ." He paused, realizing that the inevitability of the whole thing made anything else he might say a pointless prolongation of what was going to be anyway. He knew he could not say "No." He knew they really did not have anyone else to go to.

"Well?" Usery persisted.

Cal sighed. "Only until the killings are stopped—not a minute longer, Clayt. I have to insist on that."

The other man looked as if this was at least as good as he'd hoped for, and maybe better. But strangely, he did not look relieved. All he said was, "Fair enough, Cal. We can't ask any more of you than that," but it was plainly not the only thing he had on his mind.

"What is it, Clayt?" Cal asked. "There is something else, isn't there?"

There was an exchange of glances between the man and his wife—one seemingly looking for support, the other giving it—before Usery went on to explain, "Yes, there is something —something Cora and I have talked about and have decided has probably been kept secret too long already." He looked steadily at each person around the room, but mostly and finally at Cal. "It's had one hell of a repercussion on me personally, Cal, but maybe even more, now, on all of us. It's something you already know about—something Celsa Jaramillo told you a week ago—but I'd like you to hear my view of it, too. I think it may have a lot to do—maybe everything to do—with these killings."

Cal knew instantly what he was talking about, and he wondered just as quickly both how and when Clayt had learned of his conversation with Celsa. With a slight pang of guilt over this, he looked from Jenny to Caleb, noted their expressions of perplexed curiosity, and then back to Usery.

"Clayt, you don't have to . . . I mean—"

But the other man waved him off before he could finish. "I know, I know. But it doesn't matter. Celsa came to me too, this afternoon, you see. She told me everything she told you. And I understand how that came about, so I'm not angry about it. My only regret is that she didn't come to me sooner. There are certain things I didn't know and . . . well, I've done a lot of suffering, thinking some of it was more my fault than it really ever was. It might have saved me a lot, had I known."

Cal studied him. "The part about Quentin," he concluded. "All this time you really never knew?"

"No—never," Usery confirmed sadly. "Cassie never let on, and neither did Quentin. What's always been a great source of shame for me is even greater now. The kind of thing to destroy a man eventually if he doesn't come clean with at least those who count." Again he looked at his wife. "I'll curse myself forever for not doing that little chore before now."

It was Caleb who said then, "Clayt, I don't figure I know what the devil it is you're talking about, but I want to say you don't have to tell me or Jenny here if you don't want to.

You're welcome to talk to Cal in private. All you have to do is say the word. We'll understand."

Usery studied him contemplatively for several seconds before finally saying, "I don't reckon we've seen eye-to-eye on some things in the past, Caleb, and we've never really been close friends, so I don't presume to make you a personal confidant against your will. But this thing has affected this whole town, and you're a part of that as much as anybody else. It's up to you, of course, but I'm not asking that you leave—either of you. Fact is, I'd just as soon you stayed. Dirty linen or no, a little soul baring is liable to do me good. I'm not out to spread it around, you understand, but I'd just as soon you heard it from me as someone else."

Caleb and Jenny exchanged glances, and after a moment Caleb said, "Okay, Clayt, bare away. But just remember: You're talking to a newspaperman. It doesn't come natural to me to keep secrets, you know."

Usery smiled sort of weakly. "I know," he said. Then he began, "You see, one of the reasons I believe Guthrie McGuire came back to haunt this town the way he has, is what happened to his wife after he left. I can only guess how it happened, but I think he learned while he was still in prison of her death and of the fact that she may even have been driven to it. Maybe he did or didn't know that she was also driven, briefly at least, into whoredom in order to stay alive, and that finally she became a kept woman, not just by one but by two men, at least one of whom did not know about the other. I was one of those two men, the one who didn't know. To my everlasting shame, the other was my own brother Quentin."

He paused once again, this time amid the rather shocked expressions of Caleb and Jenny. Even Cal, who had learned nothing yet that he didn't already know, was silent.

Presently Usery went on, "Like I say, I don't really see how McGuire could have known all of this. Even I didn't know it all. But he must have known that his wife's fate was an unhappy one, and as I think about it he may even have known of her short, pitiful career as a prostitute. Men carry that kind of story, I'm sad to say, wherever they go . . . even into prison cells. It's perfectly plausible that McGuire heard at least that much as well as of her death later on. I also think it plausible—although maybe less than rational— that he came back to exercise his revenge on this town, killing at random, or however, until he's caught and can kill no more. I and my brother Quentin are as responsible for that as anyone else, maybe more so."

He paused again, and Caleb asked, "Cal, you already knew of this?"

Cal nodded. "Since this time last week—the night before Quentin's horse came in with blood on its saddle. It was also the night before Tom Rudabaugh showed up in town with the news that McGuire had not been killed up near Las Vegas, as had been reported earlier."

"And it explained all the things that made your earlier suspicions sound so impossible," Caleb marveled. "Cal, you stumbled onto the truth a long time before it could be believed. You deserve some credit for that, I'll say!"

"Stumbled is the word," Cal remarked to this. "And credit's due only when our killer's brought to ground. I've done no good at all along those lines."

Caleb turned back to Usery. "Why didn't you come forward with this sooner, Clayt?"

Usery wagged his head. "I didn't have any idea it mattered. Like you, like everybody, I guess . . . I couldn't believe McGuire was still alive. When we learned that and after Cal was shot, why, we went right out after him. I didn't know of Quentin's involvement. I was never able to believe that Cassie—McGuire's wife—actually took her own life. Not until Celsa came to me today. Not until I'd learned that miserable part of the story for myself."

Caleb looked for several seconds as if still struggling to come to grips with what he was hearing. Finally he said,

"Clayt, like you say, you and I haven't always seen eye-to-eye about things. I've even taken you to task about some of them in my paper on occasion. But I've never accused you of being anything other than an honorable, decent man. I find it hard to believe that you in any way drove that woman to her death. And I'll be darned if I can imagine how you ever wound up in such a situation. Quentin, maybe . . . but you!"

"No man is wholly honorable, Caleb. But I swear to all of you, I never meant to hurt that woman. At first I felt sorry for her, and a little responsible. They were my cattle McGuire stole, and it was largely me who made sure he was brought to justice. I made sure he was caught and tried, and yes, by damn, sentenced for what he did. And then this town turned its head on the woman he left behind. A good woman who wound up in the back rooms of the Pioneer Saloon, then later entertaining miners and cowboys in her own house. A woman both ruined and scorned. At first I only felt sorry for her, tried to help her. Then I fell in love with her. I thought I was pulling her up out of the gutter. It was impossible that she marry me—her husband was still alive if nothing else, and she knew her reputation would never let her function normally as any man's wife again in this town, might even destroy the man's. I kept her—in secret, of course—and I never knew when Quentin came on the scene, never understood what that did to her. Never until today."

"But what on earth would make her take up with Quentin? What kind of woman would do such a thing?"

"She was a very frightened, confused woman, Caleb. And Quentin could charm the shell off a turtle, you know that. He had no scruples about such things. It must have caused Cassie tremendous guilt, and Celsa has always maintained that in the end she took her own life as a result. Like I said, I never believed that until now."

"That's a hell of a thing to have to tell about your own

brother, Clayt," Caleb said after a moment. "Even now that he's probably dead."

"That's just it. That's one reason I'm telling it. We don't know for sure he's dead. The man we buried today may not have been my brother. And you must know by now that Quentin hated me, has for a long time. Why else would he have done something like he did? He used me too. Surely you all must have noticed the strain it put on me this past year, the power Quentin began to wield that I couldn't control." He looked at Cora. "It almost ruined my marriage, the guilt I felt, the terrible mood it put me in for so long. Only a good and understanding woman could have abided any of it, could so quickly come to give me another chance when she learned of all this."

"If only you had told me sooner, Clayt," Cora said. "How much suffering it would have saved you!"

"I was a fool—no question about that. But that doesn't change the situation as it stands now. . . ." He switched his gaze from Cora to Cal and Caleb. "What I'm saying is, my brother was long consumed with hatred. It goes back a long way, to our childhood—his rather, I guess, since I'm so much older. He always resented my being the leader, my success, which he could never quite duplicate for himself. I never wanted to admit it, but I think it actually drove him a little insane." Again he looked around. "What I'm saying is, if my brother is alive, if that man we buried wasn't him, or if the blood on that horse's saddle wasn't his, then he is a dangerous man. I'm saying that hatred may have found an outlet now that is beyond any of us to ever control again."

Even Cal was aghast at this. "Clayt, are you thinking it might have been Quentin who shot at me instead of McGuire?"

"I'm not saying that, because I don't have a way under the sun of knowing. But you remember the circumstances of Quentin's disappearance. You whipped him in a fight, in front of a crowd. I backed you. And I'll guarantee you, if he lives and for as long as he lives, he'll never forgive either of us for that. I'm saying if he's still alive out there somewhere, he's just as dangerous as Guthrie McGuire ever was."

Cal stared at him for a long several seconds. "Clayt, I wouldn't argue with you about any of this—except for one thing. I just can't believe it wasn't Quentin we buried today. I can't believe we'll ever see your brother alive again."

Usery sighed. "Well, as bad as it may sound, I guess I almost hope you're right. But I'm still not sure you are. And I've told you my story. It's pretty grimy, I know, and I'm sorry, Jenny, that you had to hear it. But now maybe you'll at least understand how things are. And I hope you'll all keep it a thing among just us. I've bared my soul pretty thoroughly here, but I don't know if I want to stand before the whole town and do it. It would only hurt Cora, and God knows I've got enough to make up to her already."

Cal, Jenny, and Caleb traded glances before Caleb spoke for all of them. "I don't think you'll have to worry about that, Clayt. Our telling would serve no purpose, and there are enough gossips and wags around this town as it is without any of us joining in to make dirt of things."

Usery rose then, to be followed in like manner by his wife and then the others. "Well, I won't take any more of your time tonight, any of you. I thank you for listening. Maybe tomorrow, Cal, we can talk about another posse. The snow's nearly melted in the open places now—maybe we'll have better luck this time. And if nothing else, by God, if it's me he wants, we'll put up signs all over these hills that all he's got to do is name the place and I'll meet him in the open."

Cora's eyes grew round at this. "Clayt! Don't you even dare consider that. Cal, don't you let him, do you hear? Don't either of you dare!"

"She's right, Clayt," Cal said seriously. "That's not a good idea."

Usery shrugged and took his coat from Caleb, who then

began helping Cora into hers. "Well, maybe it's not. We'll see. Anyhow, good night, folks. And thanks again."

As they moved toward the door, Cora told Cal in a low voice, "A lot has been explained today, Cal. A lot that you and I talked about one time, that had me so distraught and our marriage so troubled. And I'll be happier than I've ever been in my whole life. Please don't let anything happen to him now. Promise me that, Cal."

"I promise I'll try," he said.

As the door closed behind them, Caleb turned and said, "Well, how do you like that?"

"Quite a story, all right," Cal agreed.

"Yeah. And I promised not to print a word of it!"

2

A short while later, after Caleb had excused himself to go to bed, Cal and Jenny stood in the hallway next to the parlor preparing to say good night.

"Well, are you glad or not that you stayed to hear that?" Cal asked.

She looked thoughtful, almost wistful, as she considered it. "I'm not sure. I've never heard anyone reveal anything like that about himself before. Mostly, I guess it worries me to think about Quentin maybe being on the loose, going around in a dangerous frame of mind like Clayt described. I believed him, you know. That part about Quentin being a little bit insane at times. It's really frightening."

Cal gave her a quiet look of agreement but did not say anything. After a moment she asked, "What will you do now? Go back into the hills again like Clayt suggested?"

"Probably," he said. "It hasn't done a lot of good so far, but it's better than waiting around for our man to come to us. Every time that happens, someone dies. And whoever he is, he's still shooting at people. This bandage on my head is proof enough of that."

She gave a little shiver at his words. "You think he'll strike again, then?"

"I think we have to assume that. Unless we can get to him first, I figure it's just a matter of where and against whom. And when, of course. God, if we only knew where and when!"

Unfortunately, there was no way then for them to know. Which fact was ironic in that for a certain ghostly shadow at that very moment slipping quietly through the trees only a few miles away, the answer would have been ever so simple and easy to give.

3

The next day dawned as pretty and mild as any since the second snowstorm, and was so deceptively lacking in portent that Cal's whole outlook became almost euphoric as he stepped out on the walk in front of the Manor House following breakfast a couple of hours later. Already the sun was sending down warm rays that although not unusual for even a mid-November morning in this part of the country, were such a decided departure from what had gone not too many days before that it was difficult at best to believe anything but good could come of it. It appeared the height of a mild spell that, in Cal's estimation, was as badly needed as any had ever been.

The scene about town reflected this feeling clearly. The snow, except for north-facing slopes and shaded canyon bottoms, where stubborn patches would continue to persist for days, was nearly gone; Main Street, although still badly rutted, was the hardest and driest it had been since the first storm; and for the first time in days all of the shift wagons for the Glory Be and Silver Brick mines went out on schedule, loaded with miners actually anxious to get back into their normal routine. Even the Victorio, which was an eastern-owned property and much more loosely managed than the bigger two, was apparently back in business full-scale. And the stage, sitting docilely in front of the stageline office just now, appeared destined to originate its first run in over a week.

All of which was good news for Cal to ponder as he rolled a cigarette and stood for several moments mentally planning out his day. His concentration was presently broken, however, by a light step on the walk behind him. He turned to see Cora Usery standing there, looking very fresh and pretty, and happier than he had seen her in a long time.

"Good morning, Cal. Sorry I missed you at breakfast."

Cal smiled. "What's up? Taking a day off?"

"I've been upstairs getting a few of my things together," she said. "I'm moving back across the arroyo, remember? All I need is someone to help me carry some stuff. . . . Cal, it's mostly lightweight things; do you think Jenny would mind? She's such a sweet girl, and we've really never had a chance to get well acquainted. It would give us a chance to visit. You know, talk a little girl talk. Things like that."

"I'm sure she'd be tickled pink," he said, kind of pleased with the prospect himself. "Why don't you go on up and ask her?"

"Do you think it's too early?"

"Eight-thirty, too early? Around the Caleb Harvey house? Not hardly, if my experience proves anything."

"Then I will," Cora said happily. "I just will, right this minute. And, Cal, thank you again for last night. You have no idea what a lift that was for Clayt, to have the three of you simply listen. His burden may not be completely lifted, but it is lightened immeasurably, and he was like a new man afterward, believe me."

"That's great, Cora. It really is. By the way, where is he

now? I was thinking of talking to him a little later if I could find him."

"Well," she said, thinking, "he ate breakfast with me about an hour ago; then I think he was going down to the house for something, I don't remember what. Maybe it was some bookwork he's been needing to do. Anyway, I suspect he'll be there for a while. I'll tell him you'll be over if you'd like."

"That would be fine, Cora. See you later, then."

He watched her move away in the direction of the Harveys', then turned and walked the few steps next door, to the doc's house. Inside, he asked for Earl Youngblood, and found the old lawman in his room, buckling up a suitcase in preparation for catching the stage for Socorro.

"I was gonna look you up before I left, boy. I didn't want you to think I was runnin' out on you. You understand that, don't you?"

"I understand," Cal said. "Clayt told me all about it. I only wanted to see you before you left, to say good-bye and good luck. You've given this town probably a lot more than it's given you, and nobody blames you for looking out for yourself."

"Well, I just wish I could've been more help to you with this deal you got facing you. It's a pretty rotten kinda thing for any lawman to handle, much less for someone just tryin' to fill in."

"I'll vouch for that," Cal said glumly. "Any words of wisdom before you leave? Ideas of what I might do next?"

The other man considered this very seriously for several seconds before finally saying, "Not much, I'm afraid. Just don't take anything for granted and don't let your guard down even for a minute. Something will eventually happen, and if thirty years of experience has taught us anything at all, it'll come right when you least expect it. Remember that, or you'll get caught with your pants around your ankles just when you need most to run.

"Sorry I can't give you any better advice than that, but if you'll remember it you'll be prepared when you need to be— and *that* is about all you can do, believe me."

Outside, in front of the doc's house a few minutes later, Cal turned the marshal's words over in his mind without feeling either encouraged or discouraged. Then, after a moment, he sighed and stepped down from the walk, angling across in the direction of the jail. Since being shot, he had made relatively few appearances there, and he had an idea what kind of mood old Enos was likely to be in if he went on being ignored much longer.

In this prediction, he was not disappointed.

"Well, well," the jailer remarked sarcastically as he hobbled in from the back room, "must be the prodigal marshal come back to work. Was beginnin' to wonder if I'd ever again see the day."

Cal, ignoring the sarcasm, hung his hat and coat on the rack and went over to his desk. "I just said good-bye to Earl over at the doc's," he said. "You know he was leaving?"

Enos grunted. "Yeah, I knew. He was by last night for a few minutes. Guess you're it now, huh?"

"Guess so," Cal replied, slightly distracted of a sudden. Out the window he had just caught a glimpse of Cora Usery and Jenny, each with an armload of things, as they trudged past the *Myriad* on their way to the Usery home beyond the arroyo.

"Any idea yet who the man you buried yesterday was?" Enos was asking now.

"Huh? Oh . . . ideas, no conclusions."

The old jailer wagged his head. "Fine thing, if you ask me. Now, not only don't we know who the killer is for sure, we can't even figure out who's been killed!"

Cal sighed wearily. "We thought we knew. And I'm still not convinced we don't. It's just a matter of finding him."

"That posse thought they'd found his hideout," Enos said to this. "Good place to start lookin' again, if you ask me.

'Specially now most o' this snow's melted off. 'Course, that don't mean it's gonna stay off long. There's another storm comin' already, you know."

Cal, who was now idly rummaging through a pile of mostly meaningless papers on his desk, looked up. A skeptical look crossed his face.

"Don't believe me, huh? Well, just you looky here." Enos hobbled over to the windowsill across the room from Cal, and from it collected a jar filled with some sort of cloudy liquid. He hobbled back across the room. "Know what that is?"

Cal shook his head.

"It's bear grease. Plain ol' ordinary bear grease. Best way o' predictin' the weather there ever was."

Cal blinked. "Bear grease?"

"Hell yes! Looka here. See how it's all clouded up? Little flakes o' stuff all floatin' around just like snow in the air? See that? Means a storm a-comin', sure as you ain't old enough to hold my lariat rope while I pee. Yessir. Started cloudin' up yesterday—which is exactly what it'll start doin' outside this afternoon or tonight. May even be a few clouds buildin' out there now."

Cal, as much as he would have liked to, could not resist a glance out the window. Sure enough, despite what had been solidly blue sky less than an hour ago, a few high, thin clouds had formed. Not yet looking much like storm clouds . . . but clouds nevertheless. He looked back at Enos and shook himself. Bear grease!

"Still don't believe me, huh? Well, you'll see. I been watchin' my bear grease for years now. It's an old mountain man's trick, and by God it works! Yessir. Good weather a-comin', and the grease is clear, all that white stuff settlin' to the bottom just harmless as can be. But let bad weather threaten, and she'll cloud up like nobody's business. And snow . . . well, just look at the flakes. This un' may even be the worst storm yet."

Cal remained skeptical, yet could not deny a slight uneasiness as well. After a moment's thought, he rose and crossed to the hat rack. "Well, one way or the other, there's no use my putting what I've got to do off any longer. I'm going out to see about putting together another posse. I want to talk to Clayt first, then—"

He had his hat donned and his coat half on when he heard the sound. A dull, muffled pop that during less anxious times he might have thought was maybe a door slamming. But then a second pop followed closely on the heels of the first, and he turned back to Enos.

"Did you hear that?"

"What? Hell, I didn't hear nothin'. . . ."

"Damn!"

Cal disappeared outside, and as he did the old jailer muttered disbelievingly, "Now what the hell?" and hobbled on over to the window to look out, almost dropping the bear grease jar as he went and cursing all the louder for it.

4

Cal collared the first person he came to outside. It was an old man he didn't even know but who seemed to have heard the sounds just as Cal had.

"Gunshots," the old man said simply.

"Where did they come from? Could you tell?"

The old-timer pointed in the general direction of the school, the arroyo, and even more specifically the Usery home beyond, the latter fact giving Cal an almost instant sense of icy foreboding.

"Are you sure?" he demanded roughly, at the same time looking around for other bystanders who might have heard.

The old man glared at him. "I said so, didn't I?"

Several others were looking in the same direction, and Cal determined not to linger any longer. Leaping from the boardwalk, he crossed the street at a run. Dashing past a surprised Caleb Harvey standing in front of the *Myriad*, he cut between the newspaper office and Caleb's house and scrambled madly across the arroyo. All caution aside, he was already at the outer gate that was the entrance to the walled-in front yard when he ran into Carlos, one of Usery's servants, coming from inside.

The Mexican's face was ashen, and he appeared breathless. "It is Señor Clayt—he has been shot! Please hurry, *señor!*"

"Go get the doc," Cal ordered, and made for the front door, which was located in the center of a long portico that extended from end to end along the middle wing. The door stood open, flung wide, probably by Carlos as he made his exit only moments before.

Even as he entered, Cal detected the still-acrid odor of gunsmoke, and realized that once again he had been incautious in his approach. He stopped just inside the door, to look up and down the darkened hallway that stretched to either side. He was waiting for his eyes to adjust when suddenly he heard a sound coming from behind an open doorway across the hall to his left.

It sounded like a woman's voice, and was answered a moment later by what sounded like a second woman's voice. Cal quickly moved across the hall, six-gun drawn, and flattened himself against the wall. Carefully, he looked inside the room.

On the floor, sprawled full-length on his back, lay Clayton Usery. At his side, kneeling, were Cora and Carlos' wife, Juanita. The two women were ministering to the fallen Usery desperately. His shirt was open and his head rested on some sort of hurriedly fashioned pillow. Even from where Cal stood, he could see blood all over the man's chest, and he appeared to be unconscious. Juanita had a pan of water, and Cora was trying to bathe the wound—or wounds —with a damp cloth.

She looked up suddenly and saw him standing there. "Cal! Oh Cal! He—he's hurt badly. I sent Carlos for help. . . ."

"I know," Cal said, coming quickly to her side. "I met him outside. How bad is it?"

"Oh—I don't know. . . ." She moaned. "Juanita . . . here, more water on this cloth, please. Oh . . . and a dry cloth, too! I must stop the bleeding from this one! See, Cal—he's shot twice! Here . . . and here!"

"Hold that cloth tight against the wound," he told her. "You'll never stop the bleeding if you don't." He watched as she did what he told her, then asked, "Cora, who shot him? And where is Jenny?"

Her eyes flew up to meet his. "Oh Cal . . . *he's* got her! He shot Clayt and he took Jenny."

Cal stared at her with an intentness that would ordinarily have wilted a branding iron. "*Who, Cora? Who's got Jenny?*"

There were tears in her eyes as she answered, "I don't *know* who he was, Cal. Oh it was terrible. He must have slipped into the house without anyone knowing. Juanita and I were down the hall putting up some things, and Jenny was on her way back to the hotel; Clayt was here, in his study. Suddenly we heard shots, and when we got here a man stood in the hallway with his arm around Jenny's throat. He was bearded and it was too dark to tell who he was. He told us not to come any closer, then dragged Jenny toward the east wing, where they disappeared. We found Clayt lying here a few seconds later. . . ." Her words ended in a sob.

Cal, his mouth set in a grim line, stood. "You stay with Clayt," was all he said.

Back in the darkened hallway he found that his eyes adjusted quickly. He was almost certain that no one lurked between him and the east wing. Nevertheless, he made his way cautiously, calculating the possibility of someone attempting to hide or barricade himself in the house. It was a large, rambling structure, especially on the east side, where the least activity normally occurred. All of the active living quarters, except for those of the servants, were in the west wing, or in the middle, and most of the rooms to the east were either empty or used for storage. Plenty of room for hiding, no question about that.

He rounded the corner that took him into the east wing carefully, once again his back flattened against the wall, and was startled to see bright light coming from the far end of the corridor. A door to the outside stood wide open, and it caused Cal to hesitate in uncertainty. Had someone gone out? Or were they hidden inside any one of the several darkened rooms that lined the hall? A clever ruse, or a legitimate sign of their having left the house entirely?

It would have caused him an insufferable pause, the uncertainty of this, had he not suddenly seen movement through the doorway, some distance behind the house. Someone running? He wasn't sure. But then he heard the scream, and he was sure it was Jenny. Still cautious, but less so now than before, he made his way quickly down the hall to the open doorway and looked out.

Peering into hazy-bright sunlight, he at first saw nothing but the wooded hillside behind the house. Then another scream, more like a shriek actually, brought his attention to a thick oak motte about a hundred yards away. He almost made a move in that direction, but a gunshot rang out and something splintered the doorjamb within a foot of his head. Instinctively he hit the ground and rolled for the nearest cover—a small bush growing against the back wall of the house about ten feet away. He came up in a crouch, gun in hand, peering intently once more at the oak motte. Suddenly, bursting out of the oaks and into the trees beyond, came two riders sitting double astride a mount that Cal thought could only be Guthrie McGuire's spotted mule!

He couldn't tell from such a distance who the man was,

but obviously it was Jenny, her long blond hair streaming behind her, on the mule with him. And there was no way he could risk a shot. Helplessly, gun hand hanging loosely at his side, he watched as they disappeared in the dense junipers and oak brush that covered the hillside all the way to its top.

TEN

A DESPERATE TRAIL

1

Cal's stunned immobility lasted only a matter of seconds before his thoughts turned to action. He had to get a horse—his horse, any horse; he had to follow the spotted mule. Every moment spent doing anything else was a moment lost, a moment wasted.

Whirling, he raced back through the house, where at the front door he met Doc Wagner, Jeremy Chance, and Caleb Harvey, just arriving.

"What's happened?" Caleb asked. "Carlos said Clayton Usery has been shot, and something about Jenny. . . ." He looked around anxiously. "Cal, where is Jenny?"

"She's gone, Caleb. The man—whoever it was who shot Clayt—grabbed her and took off with her. . . ."

Caleb's expression became one of horrified disbelief. "My God, you can't mean that!"

"I'm afraid I can, Caleb," Cal told him. "I'm going after them right now. They took off on McGuire's mule just a few minutes ago." He looked at Jeremy. "I've got to have a horse, Jeremy."

"Your horse is over at my livery corral—right where those cowboys who brought you in last week left him," the hostler offered. "He's probably close as any . . . unless you want to take a chance on the one or two standing at hitching rails along Main Street. Or on one of Clayt's, out back."

Cal's decision was instantly and instinctively the one of any man long associated with horses: When the chips are down, go with a known quantity. Just any horse found on the street, or in another man's corral, might not have the bottom—the stamina and wind—of Cal's own grulla. And in a chase, this quality might mean all, even more than speed.

Again he addressed Jeremy. "Is my saddle and rifle at your place too?"

"On the rack just inside the door."

"Good. Clayt is just inside the study there. You men help look after him. I'm going after Jenny."

"Hey . . . wait!" Jeremy called after him. "Don't you want someone to go with you?"

But he was gone, and the three men looked at each other for a moment in absolute uncertainty. Then Doc Wagner said, "Well, c'mon. Let's go see about Clayt. He may need a lot more help than Cal does, and ain't no use you two standing around with your mouths open. No use in that."

2

Cal picked up the tracks twenty minutes later at just about the point where he had last seen the mule and its riders going through the trees. First located in mud, the imprints were then found passing through small patches of remnant snow, and finally crossing open ground that had a soft, freeze-thawed surface that left the tracks distinct and easy to follow. They led generally eastward following the ridge slope on a gradual uphill angle that finally came out on top, and from there headed straight down the ridge, still going east.

Slightly nettled by this, Cal followed the trail a good half a mile before finally deciding that his quarry was not going to cut back toward the Black Range.

A mile farther and Cal reined his grulla to a stop. He had

ridden out onto a point, below which the ridge sloped
steeply toward lower ground. Veering to one side, a lightly
used livestock and game trail curled downward, leaving the
ridge and winding its way onto a grassy bottom, where it
disappeared from Cal's view. It did not cease to attract his
attention, however, for on it, where it left the ridge, were
the mule tracks. He remained somewhat puzzled by their
course.

Briefly he considered the situation. From the time he had
last seen his quarry behind Clayton Usery's home to the moment he had picked up the tracks, he calculated that as
much as thirty minutes had elapsed. The tracks told him
that the mule had initially left out at a run or a gallop but
had soon been pulled back to a high cantor or a steady trot—
a ground-gaining pace calculated no doubt to save the mule
but at the same time to put as much ground as possible between its riders and whatever pursuers were to follow. It
was also a pace that Cal, no matter how easy the tracks were
to read, could not hope to match and track, too. By now, he
figured he could easily have lost an additional fifteen minutes, maybe even more.

This did not worry him so much in itself. The mule was
carrying double, and Cal knew that over the long haul it
would never outlast his grulla and certainly could not out-
run it. As long as he stayed steadily on the trail and did not
lose the tracks, he knew he would eventually catch up—that
is, unless they found a change of mounts someplace, or
picked up an extra one somehow. And of course there was
the chance he might lose the trail. So far nothing had been
done to hide it, but that didn't mean something couldn't,
and it certainly would be a way of slowing him down.

Then he thought: If only he had some idea where they
were headed, some way to outguess them and ride straight
on without having to make sure he didn't lose the tracks.
But he knew there was no chance of this. It was the thing
that puzzled him most, in fact. If the man who had Jenny

was indeed Guthrie McGuire (and Cal wasn't taking any bets either way now), then he was apparently quitting the mountains, maybe altogether. And what might that mean? Had he completed his revenge? And was he escaping the country with Jenny as his hostage, his prize, or both?

He shivered at this thought and renewed his study of the scene before him. The grassy bottom, he knew, presently broke out into the open valley of what was called Cuchillo Negro Creek, tributary to the Rio Grande some thirty or forty miles to the east. The Cuchillo Negro was named after an Apache warrior otherwise known as Black Knife, and was also commonly referred to as Cuchillo Creek, or sometimes simply "the Cuchillo."

At the moment, Cal's sole concern, however, was the narrow valley's import, if any, to his present situation. Mainly, he figured, it was something open that had to be crossed if his quarry were to continue on an easterly course; for along this stretch of its length, the Cuchillo ran almost due south, and he knew this pattern continued for several miles, all the way past the small mining towns of Fairview (later to be called Winston) and Chloride, to its confluence with Monument Creek, after which it cut sharply eastward and continued in that general direction until it emptied into the Rio Grande. From there south it was seventy-five miles to Las Cruces and Mesilla, and just over a hundred to El Paso and Mexico.

Which fact presented another possibility to a traveler with any of those destinations in mind—that of simply following Cuchillo Creek all the way to the big river. In some ways it was the more natural route to take, for to cross the Cuchillo at a point generally straight ahead from where Cal now sat would mean one last, small, but rugged range of mountains, not impassable by any means for horseback travelers, but much slower in the long run for most.

Either way, beyond these mountains the foothills gave way rapidly to a creosotebush- and mesquite-dotted desert, lower country, flatter and in some ways easier going, but also creased and abruptly broken by desert washes and canyons, some of which were easily as difficult to negotiate as anything the mountains had to offer.

So the question remained: Which way would Jenny's captor take, if either? Would he head south to Mexico, or might he even swerve north into the San Mateos and the Magdalenas? And from there Socorro, Santa Fe, or no telling where beyond?

Or, complicating matters even more, what if the man decided to lie in ambush and simply wait for his pursuers to appear? Assuming there were not too many—and thankfully he had no way of knowing that—all he had to do was leave a trail out across open country, pick a spot with good cover on high ground, and lay down on them as they came into the open. Enough to give anyone about to cross open ground pause for a second thought, no question about it.

To further add to all this, Cal could not erase from his mind old Enos' warning about the weather. No matter what he thought about the bear grease theory, there was that unmistakable feeling in the air now: high clouds increasing and lowering, a cold moistness, a certain smell in the air, an absolute stillness that was now more like a lull before than a break after. . . .

To Cal's relief, he found that the tracks did not immediately cross open ground. At the foot of the ridge they left the trail entirely and stayed with the light tree cover of the ridge slopes all the way to the dry bed of the Cuchillo. From there it was straight across the narrow valley—strictly ignoring the road north from Fairview—up and across the low, rolling hills that fronted the small mountain range beyond, and then into the mountains themselves, where the trail swerved sharply south and east in what Cal thought was a true indication now of his quarry's destination: the distant, winding ribbon that was the Rio Grande!

Cal's problems were not solved by this knowledge, however. It was still a big country; there were too many different routes to follow to get to a place. And there were still the foothills south of Fairview that a man being hotly pursued might turn to once the mining towns were skirted. The only thing about this was, that's probably where the most people were. From Fairview and Chloride south were the other towns: Hermosa, Hillsboro, Kingston; and from one to the other, the hills were teeming with miners. And quite obviously Cal's quarry did not want to be seen. The desert, although not entirely unpopulated, would certainly offer the better chance of going undetected.

Yet even in light of this reasoning only two things really remained certain: One, Cal had no choice but to continue tracking; and two, the tracks were suddenly becoming much harder to follow.

He didn't attribute this latter circumstance to any special effort made on his quarry's part; picking the easiest and fastest way of going still seemed that party's main concern. It was just that the country was rougher now, and the farther one got from Grafton and the other towns, the taller the grass, the fewer the trails. Of course, when they did happen to hit on one, the mule tracks were less likely to be confused with horse tracks, for what trails there were had been made and used largely by game. Even then, Cal was having a time of it. By shortly after noon he had gone little more than five miles—mostly southward—from where he had left the Cuchillo Negro, and he still had not left the mountains. He paused atop a high saddle, both to let the horse blow and to survey what lay ahead.

He figured himself to be as much as an hour to an hour and a half behind now, as his own going had been so laborious at times as to bring him to a virtual crawl, and only twice had he found sign of his quarry having stopped. Once, he had observed footprints, one set of which he decided were Jenny's leading toward a bush off to one side; the other time there had been a good deal of milling of the mule tracks mixed with the two sets of human prints—the mule being rested most likely. To be sure, there had been a couple of hard climbs already, which had taken a lot out of the grulla and he hoped even more out of the mule—his one hope that he might not be so far behind after all and that he might soon even begin to catch up.

But then there was the weather—ever darkening, becoming ominous now, the sun disappearing in the clouds, the air becoming colder, and a brisk breeze beginning to whip from out of the north. . . .

Once again he looked ahead. He was facing almost due east, but his vantage was magnificent to either side as well as straight ahead. To his left and slightly behind him was Iron Mountain; also on his left but more to the fore and farther away was the southern end of the San Mateos, and at their foot the meandering valley of the Cañada Alamosa. Straight ahead, the desert, the snakelike ribbon cutting north and south that was the Rio Grande, the abrupt profile of the Fra Cristobal Mountains just east of the river, and beyond that, becoming indistinct with the lessening visibility of the day, the broad, flat plain of the dreaded Jornada del Muerto. Farther yet hove the Sierra Oscura and the northern end of the jagged San Andres. To his right, the footslopes of Cuchillo Mountain, about five miles away, and the Cuchillo Negro cutting its way eastward now, down into the creosotebush flats above the Rio Grande. Out of sight within the Cuchillo's bottom was the tiny Mexican village of the same name, as was that of Monticello, farther north within the canyon of the Alamosa.

And nowhere was there a soul or thing to be seen moving. No rider or riders on a spotted mule, no birds flying, no cattle or deer moving about. Nothing at all that he could see.

He sighed and looked back at the tracks on the ground. For the last couple of miles the trail had led generally eastward, but now it seemed to be turning south again—the in-

tention apparently being to leave the mountains but at the
same time to hug their juniper-smattered footslopes for as
long as possible before breaking out onto the desert. And as
yet there was no clear sign of faltering on the mule's part;
the sure-footed animal seldom dragged its feet and had
rarely stumbled even while crossing the rockiest of ground.

Again Cal sighed. He wished there was some way for him
to hurry his end of the chase. He wished he were not so hungry and that he had had time to pack some food—even a few
chunks of brittle jerky would have been welcome—anything.
And he wished it were not so cold, that the sun had not
been blotted out so totally by dark clouds, that what he had
not thought possible in the weather only a few hours ago
was not so undeniably imminent now. He wished a lot of
things . . . and knew at the same time that wishing was the
last thing that would do him any good.

His sense of urgency ever mounting now, he once again
turned the grulla onto the trail, and for the first time felt
tiny bits of moisture pelting him from behind.

3

Less than five miles away, the objects of Cal's pursuit also
felt the moisture in the air. Misery showed plainly on their
faces as they rode the tiring mule, sitting stiffly, their backs
to the wind, the man behind the girl yet each with limbs already becoming numb from the combined cold and inactiv-
ity. For over an hour now, they had not even spoken, there
being little that was of a common ground for them to talk
about, and those last words having been a mere grudging
acceptance by the girl of a blanket from the man's bedroll to
protect her from the cold and the wind. Beyond that, neither had evidenced any good thoughts toward the other's
welfare, nor did either have much reason for doing so.

The man's main concern, in fact, was the mule. He never

doubted that he was being pursued. But he had also reasoned that whoever his pursuers were, they must have gotten a poor start, else they would have run him down long ago. They were having to track him. Slowly, painstakingly . . . well, maybe not so painstakingly as he would have liked, for in his haste to build a lead he had banked so heavily on a good head start and a steady pace that he had all but ignored opportunities to cover his trail. Until now, in the desert, where it was all but impossible to do so. Too late.

But it had worked anyway . . . for a while. Then the mule had started to fade, and for the past five miles the animal had been up to no more than a walk, and rest stops were becoming necessary after every little hill, every climb out of a deep wash, every mile or so of flat ground. All of which meant that his pursuers, assuming they had not lost his trail (and he could not afford to assume that), would now be gaining ground rather than losing it . . . maybe rapidly.

He had considered getting off and walking—figured it would even help warm him up, get the blood flowing again —but precious little good it would do the mule now, or if and when he needed to make a run for it. And of course there had always been the alternative of dumping the girl. But he had been stubborn earlier and didn't want to, and now it was beginning to look more and more like he might yet need her as a hostage in the event he was overtaken. Besides, he had his own plans for her. Taking her with him had never been part of his plan, and he wouldn't have, except suddenly there she had stood, right there before him in the hallway following the shooting, her eyes wide and her expression that of total astonishment, and it had seemed so completely natural to grab her and force her to go with him. And now that he had her, well, he had no intention of giving her up. It was as simple as that.

Nevertheless, she was a burden. And the very fact that he had thus far so carefully avoided places of habitation had

equally surely prevented any opportunity to procure another mount. So there he was, stuck with a tiring mule and a
girl. Stuck.

But he still had hope. There was always the weather.
Plainly now, a storm was in the wind. Everything about the
day spelled a bad turn—the sudden change from bright and
warm to dark and cutting cold; and the wind, coming on
like death now—mean, vicious, undeniable, and beginning to
howl at times. A northerlike blast carrying with it enough
snow to cover his tracks many times over, he was sure. The
only problem was time. How soon? Would the snow beat
out his pursuers or not?

And even the weather was a two-sided coin. Just as he
hoped it would come soon enough to foil all efforts at his
pursuit, he himself could ill afford to be caught in it without
shelter. And here again he had a problem. He knew generally where he was—somewhere north of Cuchillo Negro
Creek, maybe as much as five miles still, and better than
twice that from the little town of Cuchillo—and he was
headed for the Rio Grande, hoping to skirt Cuchillo to the
west and south, then strike the river and head south for El
Paso and Mexico. All this was fixed in his mind like rock in a
mountainside. But precisely where he was right now and
where shelter might be found was more guess than anything
else. He had been to Cuchillo only once, two years ago, and
then had used a different route to get there; and he had
never been down the Rio Grande to the south. He simply
was not that familiar with his surroundings.

Yet he did know that there were scattered ranches and
homesteads between here and there, and he was certain that
as many as not stood abandoned. The Apaches had seen to
that. And therein lay his hope to find shelter. An abandoned
house, shed, lean-to—anything. All he had to do was keep
the mule going, his eyes peeled, and hope. Sooner or later

something would show itself if he could just keep going. He would ride the mule right into the ground, to death, if he had to. Yes, he would.

It was not until later that he realized what he had forgotten about mules. Unlike horses, it is a rare mule that can be ridden to its death, that will give its last ounce on demand by its rider. A mule knows when it has done enough, when to call it quits. The spotted mare was as good a saddle mule as any, in many ways better than most horses. But she was still a mule.

Three miles more and she balked. In midstride almost, she stumbled once and then stopped. Vicious heels assailed her side and curses her ears, but she would not move. The man dismounted; he pulled and yanked at her reins, trying to get her to lead; he lashed her unmercifully across the hindquarters with his lariat rope. Still she would not move.

Finally he hauled the girl from the saddle and again tried to get the animal to at least lead. Then he gave the girl the reins and went back and renewed the lashing. Nothing. It was hopeless.

Cursing bitterly, he yanked his rifle from the saddle boot, what was left of his bedroll from behind the cantle, and walked around to face the mule. Amid a sudden lull in the wind, he raised the rifle.

For a moment the girl stood with a blank look on her face. Then, when she realized what he was going to do, she screamed, *"No! Oh no!"* But before she could move to interfere, he fired, and the spotted mule collapsed where it stood like an ox before the ax. The girl screamed again and broke into sobs; and then, almost as if on cue, the wind surged anew in a prolonged gust that was suddenly loaded with icy sleet, cutting and biting at their faces and forcing them to turn away.

Moments later the air was filled with driving, blinding snow.

4

But for the wind's momentary lull, Cal would never have heard the shot. As it was he must have been at least two miles away, and he couldn't be sure it was even a shot.

He had dismounted only seconds before and was in the process of studying the tracks and some fresh droppings on the trail. It was plain to him now that he was catching up quite rapidly. The tracks had some while back begun to show that the mule was beginning to stumble, to falter frequently; the droppings were the freshest he'd seen yet; and ever since he'd left the mountains the tracking had become easier and thus less cumbersome to his own pace.

Yet desperation gripped him as he realized that the snow was ever more imminent too, now; that no matter how hard he tried he yet might fail to catch up in time. And then he heard the shot—or at least what he thought was a shot. It was impossible to tell its exact direction, and he didn't even know it had anything at all to do with his quarry.

But it was something. And moments later, when the wind renewed its fury, and sleet, then snow, swirled all about him, he knew it might be his only hope. Satisfying himself that the mule tracks led in the same general direction as that of the shot, he remounted the grulla and checked what landmarks he could still see.

Nevertheless, within minutes the ground was covered with a thin blanket of white, the tracks were no more, and all he had to go on were those vague, fast disappearing landmarks, the mental echo of what he thought was a gunshot, and hope.

Jenny had two things to be thankful for: One, when Cora Usery had come to ask her help that morning, she had for some reason decided on a warm divided riding skirt and laced boots that came well up on her calves and above the hem of the skirt; the other was the blanket her captor! had given her. She had been wearing her coat and gloves when he'd come upon her there in the hallway, for she was on her way back to the hotel to get some more of Cora's things, but the coat and gloves alone would never have been enough against the viciousness of the wind and the wetness of the cold. Never.

Even so, it was a day out of a nightmare for Jenny, something her rapidly numbing, exhausted mind and body could hardly accept as real and yet could no more easily deny. No imagined misery could be so harsh, no fear so complete and terrifying. But the misery outweighed the fear right then. She was so cold she hurt; and she needed to relieve the pain in her bladder so terribly she could hardly think of anything else, yet would not say so because the last time she had later discovered that he had stood there and watched her through the bush she had gone behind. And she knew that now, in the snow, he would not let her out of his sight no matter what the reason or how hard she begged.

Not that modesty would really matter in the end, she supposed. It was a weary mind disposed to resignation that thought this, she knew; but she also knew that all they were looking for now was shelter, any kind of shelter but preferably something with a roof and four walls, a place to get in out of the snow and wind. And if they found it, she knew too what else would be in store for her. She knew what he had on his mind.

Never before in her life had she been caused to worry about being physically assaulted by a man; chivalry and decency to women were the rules rather than the exceptions in her day, even among many otherwise "bad" men. But not for this man: She could see it in his hard yet evasive eyes; she could feel it in every word he had said to her. Sooner or later, when the opportunity presented itself, he would prove it to her. No amount of naïveté could deny or ignore that, and Jenny was not a naïve woman. She knew what she knew.

Oh she would fight. She might die for it—might anyway, no matter what she did—but never would she submit quietly or meekly. There was always that chance that she would be rescued, or maybe would get his gun away from him . . . always a chance.

But nothing—time, circumstances, nothing—seemed to be on her side. It was snowing so hard now that they couldn't see more than fifty feet in any direction; and they had walked forever, it seemed. She was so tired of being shoved or dragged through and around creosotebushes, through snow now over her ankles and drifting deeper all the time, that she was almost ready to collapse. In fact, she was so miserable she was almost sick, so desperate to find shelter that all other consequences hardly seemed bad anymore.

She had been stumbling along, being partly dragged but mostly pushed, her head down and paying little attention to what was more than one step ahead, when suddenly she was yanked to a stop.

"Don't go any farther," he ordered harshly. "Look . . . don't you see? That's a straight drop-off; two more steps and you'd have gone to the bottom, head over heels."

She stared into the snowy blankness before her. It was just discernible and just as he had said, a sudden hole in the world, a gap of indistinguishable width and breadth and with no bottom she could see. "Oh my God! What is it?"

"It's a canyon," he said bitterly. "Cuchillo Negro probably. We've struck it right above the box, worst damn place of all to come up on it."

She looked up at him, failing to comprehend. "Why? What difference does it make?"

He looked at her as if she were an idiot. "Hell—look! Everything's straight down, pure rock bluffs. We couldn't climb down that on a good day, much less this one. We'll have to work our way downcanyon to find a way."

"Why do we have to go down there?"

For a moment it looked as if he was going to explain it to her, but all he finally said was, "Because I said so, that's why," and with a rough shove, he then aimed her off in the new direction.

Cal counted it little more than blind luck that he ever even saw the dead mule. He would have passed within twenty-five feet of it and never known the difference had the grulla not shied suddenly. It barely made a decent hump in the snow, and he would never have known it wasn't a rock had not one foot stuck out at an odd angle.

Only a brief inspection was needed to tell him that it was the spotted mule and that it had been shot between the eyes, probably within the half hour. The shot he'd heard almost beyond a doubt.

He looked around desperately for sign of the mule's riders but was not surprised when he found none. Whatever tracks they had made were long since covered over by snow. Again he looked into the snowy air, futilely. Then, after several seconds, he remounted the grulla and reined in the only direction that made any sense—the same one he had been following for the past hour or so. At least he hoped it was the same one. After a while in the snow he knew his chances might be no more than one in four that it was. One in four at best.

One way he would know, at least: Cuchillo Negro Canyon. If he was right, he would strike it very soon, probably within half an hour at most. If not . . . well, he could wind up almost anywhere.

It was Jenny who saw him first, and even then she thought him an apparition born of the snow and the wind. Suddenly he had loomed at them from maybe no more than thirty feet away, the man and the horse, the latter the more ghostlike of the two, for it was almost white, covered with snow that had stuck like ice to its long-haired coat, mane, and tail.

From beside her came an explosive, "Who in hell is that?" and she knew that if it was an apparition it had appeared not only to her. "*Speak up, man! Who are you?*"

"Fair question," came the reply. "Who're you?"

A tremendous thrill coursed through Jenny's veins as she recognized the voice, but then she did not know how otherwise to react to it, and apprehension and indecision gripped her. She did not have the leisure to think about it long, either, for suddenly she felt a movement at her side, then saw the rifle flash upward. Instinctively she blurted, "Cal—look out! He's going to shoot!"

But even as she cried out she knew it was too late for Cal to do anything about it; even if he already had his own gun out and ready to fire, she knew he would be afraid to shoot, afraid he might hit her. Giving it no more thought than this, and with all her might, she shoved out at her captor, driving him off balance to the side just as he fired.

To her surprise he actually went down in the snow, floundering, struggling to regain his balance. Finally he did, more or less, but as he came once again to his feet he seemed to slip, this time almost going over backward, his arms flailing and—to Jenny's virtual disbelief—the rifle flying through the air and disappearing in a world of white behind him. Desperately he looked off into the gloom, then back at his adversaries—Jenny running through the snow and getting away, Cal sitting there, his rifle leveled now. A shocked look on his face, the man simply stood there spraddle-legged, probably realizing that he had no chance if he went for his sidearm and calculating what else he might do.

For a moment he appeared to slump, as if giving up, resigned to his fate. But just as Cal started to speak, the man whirled and dove to the right, hit the snow, rolled, and amazingly vanished in the gloom beyond.

"Oh Cal, no!" Jenny cried. "*Cal . . . he got away!*" She was standing alongside the horse, her hands now on Cal's leg.

Cal's eyes were glued to the spot where he'd last seen the other man. He squinted hard into the blankness. "Jenny! Who was that man?"

She looked at him strangely. "You mean you don't know? You couldn't tell?"

"He was bearded. . . . I figured all along maybe he was McGuire. . . ."

She stared at him. "It's not McGuire, Cal. He killed McGuire up in the mountains somewhere, just like he tried to kill you and Clayt. . . . It's Quentin, Cal. Quentin Usery."

Slowly, grimly, he dismounted the grulla and handed the reins to the girl, never once taking his eyes off the spot where Usery had disappeared. "You stay with the horse. Don't go anywhere unless I call—and then only if you're sure it's me. And take this. Use it if you need it." He slipped the cold butt of his six-gun into her hand. And then he was gone.

Usery had gone over the side of the canyon, Jenny was sure of that now. The reason he had so suddenly disappeared, the canyon. Had he fallen? Or jumped? Or was it that steep here? She knew he had been looking for the slopes to become more gradual. Bluffs still, but not nearly so steep as before.

After several minutes a form took shape in front of her, coming out of the snow. Her hand tightened around the gun butt and her pulse raced, but then she knew it was Cal and she relaxed.

"He's gone, Jenny. There's a trail down there, a way down. He went off the side, probably already to the bottom by now."

"What are we going to do?" she asked fearfully.

He looked at her for a long moment. "The only thing we can do," he said finally. "It'll be dark soon; we have to have shelter. We've got no choice but to go the same way he did. Straight to the bottom of the canyon."

ELEVEN

GHOSTS NO MORE

1

They found shelter about two hundred yards back up the canyon, a shallow cave carved within the cliff face by centuries of floods. Fully protected from the wind that howled above them, they found the ground dry beneath the overhanging cliff and for several feet in front of it. They even found several small piles of driftwood deposited against the base of the cliff as if stacked there by some summer flood for just the firewood they needed. After checking the cave to make sure there were no snakes or varmints such as bobcats and skunks hidden inside, Cal unsaddled the grulla and built a fire, around which he and Jenny huddled while they watched the snow keep coming down in blankets against an ever-darkening background outside.

"He thought you dead, Cal," she told him presently. "He was the one who ambushed you that day when you were coming back to town from your homestead. It was you and Clayt he wanted. Today he thought he had succeeded with you both. Taking me with him was just cream off the top, something he hadn't planned. I think he was heading for Mexico. And Cal, I believe he really has lost his mind. There is no telling what kind of hell would have been in store for me if he'd made it."

Cal stared at the fire thoughtfully. "It explains a lot, I guess. I could never understand why I was shot at before.

McGuire didn't even know me." He wagged his head. "Still I thought maybe he was McGuire when I saw him. The beard, everything. . . . Did he say how he happened to kill McGuire?"

"Not exactly. Only enough that I gathered he had accidentally come across the man's hiding place up in the Black Range someplace—the same one the posse found, I'm sure. How he came to get the drop on McGuire, I don't know. But he did sort of say that he set it up to look like he himself was killed instead. Loaded the body on his own horse, mostly so there would be blood on the saddle, then simply let it fall back off and sent the horse home . . . knowing it would head straight for the livery in town. Then I suppose he tried to bury the body, it having occurred to him that he might even use McGuire's identity to carry out his revenge on you and Clayt. He must not have counted on it being dug up, yet I think it was only at the last, after he'd shot Clayt and kidnaped me, that he decided he couldn't get away with it and would have to leave the country."

She paused, then went on, "That's only a guess, Cal. But I know he thought he had been recognized when he shot Clayt. He knew Cora and Juanita had seen him, and me, and you as you stepped out the back just before he put me on the mule and took off. Of course, he didn't know who you were—just that you were someone who might have known him, no more. He really did think you dead, and I did nothing to let on different. I don't know why, but somehow I thought it better to just let him go on thinking he killed you. Maybe it paid off, too; I know he was so surprised to learn it was you there in the snow that he was caught almost completely off guard."

"He wasn't the only one," Cal said unhappily. "I just sat there and held my rifle while he got away."

It was plain from the look on Jenny's face that she had been thinking of this, too. She spoke soberly. "It frightens me to think about him still being out there, Cal. What's to keep him from coming back? He still has his six-gun; we wouldn't have a chance if he decided to sneak back here and murder us."

Cal thought about this with a grim mouth and a set jaw, his eyes instinctively turning to the snowy world outside the cave. If anything, it was coming down even harder than before; he doubted he or anybody else could see more than twenty-five feet, even during the lulls. He returned his gaze to the girl. "It'd have to be a pure accident for him to find us in this, Jenny. I'd never have chanced the fire otherwise. But that doesn't mean it couldn't happen. We'll have to keep our eyes open through the night. Probably too cold to sleep much anyway."

"But what about in the morning? It's bound to quit snowing sometime. What will we do then?"

Cal sighed. "That's something we'll just have to deal with when the time comes. Right now, we've got to get through the night somehow. We've got no food and a minimum of blankets. All we can do is try to survive and see."

For the first time she smiled slightly. "I suppose that will mean snuggling up a bit to keep warm. Right?"

He looked at her, startled. "I reckon it might mean that. Why?"

Her smile broadened somewhat. "Just so long as that's all it means," she said, her warning lighthearted but serious also. "So long as that's all."

2

She needn't have concerned herself; it was far too cold to worry about anything other than keeping warm, too cold even to do much sleeping. Jenny dozed off a few times, and once so did Cal. But for the most part they were awake and hungry, and cold.

As it turned out, she needn't have worried about anyone

sneaking up on them in the night, either. The wind let up shortly after dark, but not the snow. If anything, it came down even harder yet, and by morning, when it finally did taper off, better than a foot and a half had piled up on the level just outside the cave.

Daylight came gradually as the clouds continued to persist, and it found them down to the last few sticks of their firewood. Cal stepped outside and found the grulla still standing where it had been ground-tied the night before, its back humped against the cold and its coat so covered with snow that even its black mane and tail looked almost white. The snowfall had lessened to a sputter now, and visibility had cleared to several hundred yards.

Presently Jenny called out, "Well, what do you see?"

He was about to say nothing, just snow, when suddenly he did see something. It lay upcanyon about two hundred yards where the canyon narrowed abruptly in what looked like a purely vertical box. He had heard about this box, and that somewhere above flowed springs and seeps enough that through this stretch of the Cuchillo's length filled the streambed to its fullest throughout all but the driest years. Downstream it provided irrigation for the few Mexican farmers who had managed to hold their land against the Apaches; and somewhere near the mouth of the box was a small dam that diverted the water used in this irrigation into a laboriously constructed ditch system to be shared by all.

But none of this was what caught Cal's eye. Tucked in the curve in the canyon wall just this side of the box was a small homestead: two small cottonwood trees and several that looked like fruit trees, a small pole corral sticking out of the snow outback, a couple of sheds, a dilapidated outhouse with its door swung open, and sitting forlornly in the middle, a low-roofed, rock masonry house with snow drifted against its back wall almost to the roof. Most noticeable of all, however, was the fact that smoke curled lazily skyward from its chimney.

"Come and look for yourself," he told Jenny in answer to her question.

She appeared beside him, blanket wrapped about her shoulders and head, and looked in the direction he indicated.

"See anything strange about that?"

She frowned. "I don't know. There's smoke coming out of the chimney, but I don't see anything so strange about that. . . ."

Cal shook his head. "Look again. Out back—the corral, the sheds, the outhouse. Do you see anything that makes the place look lived in? Any animals, wagons, anything at all?"

She considered this for a second, then said, "No . . . except the smoke. Someone had to have made the fire. . . ." Then it came to her and a look of discernment crossed her face. "Quentin—you think it's Quentin in there?"

"I think it's possible."

Now her look was one of deep concern. "What will we do? How will we know?"

Cal, who had been wondering the same thing, found his gaze fixed on the vegetation that grew along the foot of the bluffs between the cave and the house. Shoulder to head-high arrowweed, mostly; Apache-plume, a few chamiza bushes, some mesquite, all blanketed with snow and some weighted down by it. Not the best of cover, especially with a background of pure white all around it, but cover nevertheless.

"I'm going to take a chance on being able to slip around and come up from behind," he announced finally. "I'll leave you and the horse here, and I'll leave you a gun, just in case. . . ."

"No!" she said flatly. "You can leave the horse, but you're not leaving me. I'm going with you."

"This may be dangerous, Jenny," he tried to dissuade.

"Everything that's happened to me in the past two days has been dangerous," she maintained stubbornly. "I will not be left alone."

Thoughtfully he resurveyed his intended route; it would be almost impossible for them to go undetected by whoever might be watching from the house. There was, on the other hand, adequate cover if someone decided to potshot at them; all they had to do was be careful and not get in too much of a hurry. And they could eventually get behind the house where the available cover would include outbuildings and corrals as well as vegetation. And the more he thought about it, the more he doubted that he would feel any more comfortable than Jenny if he left her alone. They didn't know for certain it was Quentin Usery in that house; and if it was not, then the man could be almost anywhere.

"Okay," he said finally, "maybe you're right. But you do what I tell you and keep me between you and that house at all times, understand?"

"I understand."

They left the horse tied beside the cave and began making their way through the snow toward the nearest stand of arrowweed. They went at a crouch and the going was not easy, but they made it without incident. Except for the smoke from the chimney, there still was no movement, nothing at all, from the house.

It had stopped snowing now, and the clouds appeared to be lifting, which only served to make it seem colder than before. Their breaths formed smokelike vapor in the air, while Cal's hands, though gloved, were becoming frozen to the grip of his rifle, and Jenny's nose and lips were almost blue—all of which made it much easier to keep going than to show the patience needed to stop and wait and watch along the way.

It took almost fifteen minutes to negotiate the first hundred yards, and at least as long to make the second. Now they were directly behind the corrals, and still there was no sign of their having drawn any notice from the house. And plainly now, the place had the look of abandonment. There were no livestock, no dogs, and long-standing inattention to the outbuildings was obvious.

Their problem was how to get close enough to see into the house. To their advantage was the snow drifted all the way to the roof along the back wall; no way anyone could see out, even if they themselves could not see in. To their disadvantage was having to put themselves in the open for the last thirty yards or so while they worked their way around to the side. If they had already been seen, this latter could present a real problem; if not, it really didn't look like it mattered.

Carefully they made their way past the outbuildings toward the left side of the house. The smoke from the chimney had slackened somewhat now, as if from a dying fire, and still there was no other sign of life from inside. Finding no window on the left side, they were forced to go on to the front. There they discovered two windows but both were boarded up, and all they could see through the cracks was darkness.

Cal handed Jenny his six-gun and told her to stay at the corner of the house, then moved toward the front door. The latch string, if there was one, was not out, and the door was tightly shut. Carefully positioning his rifle so it would be ready if need be, he put a boot against the door and shoved as hard as he could. The latch was apparently in place but still it gave enough to indicate that the wood was probably half rotten, and the bolt that held it to the door was on the verge of pulling out. One more kick should do it. Only now there could be no element of surprise, at least not from Cal's side of the door. Whoever—if anyone—was on the other side knew he was there now. It gave him pause, but he knew there was nothing he could do now but kick again.

He braced himself, then once more put his foot to the door; this time it not only gave but also swung back, kicking up dust as it dragged against a dirt floor and stopped three quarters of the way open. Cal stepped quickly back out of the possible line of fire, fully expecting gunshots to come belching his way.

But what he heard were not gunshots. An angry outburst of buzzing *whrrrs* erupted as if from a rudely disturbed hornets' nest, and for Cal it was maybe the luckiest thing that had happened to him in a month that he stepped back. He didn't need to see them to know what they were. The room was filled with rattlesnakes! And although ordinarily in almost full hibernation this time of year, this group was anything but sleepy. Carefully he moved around to where he could get a better view.

Through the door just enough daylight shone now to illuminate the fireplace and its dying fire. On the floor, everywhere he could see, were snakes, some writhing away from the light, others coiled and buzzing dangerously. And it didn't take long for him to figure out what had happened. A snake den to beat all snake dens, the rattlers had probably been congregated in a hole somewhere beneath the fireplace, cold and immobile just as they were supposed to be, when the fire had been started and its heat had eventually brought them angrily to life.

But who had started the fire?

Again Cal's eyes swept the murky interior. How he missed it the first time he didn't know, but now he thought he could make out an empty bedroll lying just a few feet from the fireplace. A split second later he located what had been its occupant. It was a sickening sight, and he had no idea that Jenny had somehow come to his side and was looking in, else he would not have let her see.

She gasped when she saw and hung onto Cal's arm for support. "Oh my God!" she moaned.

Sitting slumped against the darkened back wall about fifteen feet now from the bedroll, a look of fear-crazed agony frozen on his face, was the luckless form of Quentin Usery. From one sleeve a small rattler flopped feebly, its fangs caught hopelessly in the fabric of his coat. In one hand he still held his six-gun, and it appeared that he had managed to take at least three or four of the snakes with him. But for every one he'd shot there must have been fifty live ones, and if he had been bitten less than a hundred times it would have to have been a miracle. And because Cal was so sure of this, he was equally sure that the man was dead. He had to be.

But suddenly Jenny's fingernails were digging into his arm so hard it hurt, and she was saying, "Cal! Oh Cal . . . look at his eyes! They moved. . . . *Oh God, they moved!*"

Instinctively he put his free hand over hers, trying to quiet her, calm her. "Jenny, you're wrong. They couldn't have. He's dead. . . ."

But then, incredibly, the body seemed to jerk, the expression on the face changed, and indeed the eyes seemed to widen. Muscles bunched, and from somewhere deep inside the body the most unearthly sound Cal had ever heard a human make rose into an eerie, craze-filled scream. Then, somehow, he was coming to his feet, lurching forward, then wobbling drunkenly and falling back against the wall. The gun was still in his hand but almost surely useless now, and the other arm was being flung wildly as if it were something apart from the rest of the body, apparently in an attempt to dislodge the rattler hanging from his sleeve.

And finally the eyes, those horrible, nightmarish eyes, seemed to focus on Cal and Jenny. Once again there was a bunching of muscles, the whole remaining energy of the body being summoned for one last leap forward. Snakes buzzed and whirred and struck at his legs with lightning quickness. And he screamed again, a purely mindless scream that did not come from pain or anything else a normal mind could harbor.

"*Aaagh! Aaaaagh!*"

Instinctively Cal thumbed back the hammer of his rifle, unsure if he would shoot but somehow knowing he must be ready for anything. And then Usery started, came maybe three steps forward and, features suddenly gone slack, fell once again among the snakes. For a few moments one leg jerked slightly, but after that the body was still, completely so, and it remained out of reach from the door.

Jenny, so dumb struck she could not scream, collapsed, sobbing in Cal's arms. Presently, when she could sob no more, Cal took her and led her away, back toward the cave and the horse.

3

They found food and a place to stay a few miles down-canyon at the small village of Cuchillo, and supreme hospitality in the person of one Juan Ferdinand Chavez y Chavez, a poor but gracious farmer who, with his family, made his home at the edge of town.

Later in the day a party led by Cal and Chavez y Chavez dispatched itself to go after the body of Quentin Usery. They found the house once again cold and the rattlers, as best as they could tell from outside, having crawled back inside their hole. Nevertheless, no one felt brave (or foolish) enough to take a step inside, and thus a lariat rope was brought out and after several tosses Usery's right foot secured so the body could be dragged out through the door. Tomorrow, according to Chavez y Chavez, some of them would come back with a few charges of dynamite and put an end to the snake den. Right now, the body was to be carried back to Cuchillo and left, covered, inside a shed on the edge of town until a decision could be made as to what should be done with it from there.

It was uncertain who might make this decision but that problem was solved soon enough, shortly before dark that evening, when a party from Grafton led by Jeremy Chance and Caleb Harvey appeared at the outskirts of town asking if a man with a girl had been seen, or another man—all three

Anglos—who might have been following the first two. That
all three, one way or another, could be found right there in
Cuchillo was met with only mild surprise compared with the
astonishment that greeted their story.

"Quentin must have been asleep when the snakes came at
him," Cal told them a short while later as he finished filling
in the details. "He probably never had a chance."

Caleb Harvey wagged his head. "Well, we missed out on
a lot, I can see that. With any luck at all, we'd have been
here sooner, but it took us till noon yesterday helping Doc
with Clayt and trying to get this bunch together. Even then,
we were doing pretty good keeping on your trail, till we lost
the tracks in the snowstorm south of Iron Mountain. That
stopped us dead, let me tell you. We wound up spending the
night in the Black Range Hotel at Fairview and most of the
morning wandering around in the snow just hoping to get
lucky and spot something. Finally we decided to split up,
about half of us going on down toward Hermosa, the rest
coming here. It was pure luck we stumbled onto you at all.
And if you hadn't caught up with them, Cal, we might never
have seen Jenny again."

"Or I might have wound up in that house with Quentin,"
Jenny put in, a thought that had been giving her chills ever
since. "Dead just like he is . . . oooh!" The horror of the
idea was so great she trembled every time she thought
about it.

"How about Clayt?" Cal asked then. "How was he when
you left? He looked pretty bad, what little I saw of him."

Caleb shook his head. "Pretty bad is right. But Doc was
doing all he could, and I think maybe he'll make it. Cora
was with him, and he was conscious—enough even that he
was able to tell us it was Quentin who shot him." He
paused. "Guess you were the only one who didn't know who
you were trailing, Cal. Although I'll have to say, none of us
were quite able to believe it even after we were told. We've
had so much that was hard to believe lately: McGuire com-

ing back to haunt us when we all thought him dead; then that one himself killed by Quentin Usery—the very man so many of us thought we'd buried back in Grafton a week ago; three snowstorms the likes no one I know has ever heard of in this part of the country in two weeks; and now this deal with the rattlesnakes . . . whew! I've heard of old abandoned places like that becoming regular snake dens, but I've never heard of anything like this happening. God, what an end to a story I'll have to try to write when I get back!"

Cal smiled thinly. "Fact is stranger than fiction, isn't that what they say? People will believe most anything if you claim it's fact."

"Well, I don't know if I'd quite say that," Caleb said doubtfully. "But they'll have to believe this. No way I'd make a thing like this up. No way."

"What are we going to do with the body?" Jeremy asked then. "Take it back with us?"

"I sort of think Clayt would want us to, don't you?" Cal said. "Bad as he's been, Quentin was his brother."

On this there was general agreement, and the next morning after the sun was well up and warm in the sky, the party left out on its way back to Grafton with the body slung across the back of a packhorse. Cal and Jenny, riding double astride the hardy grulla, hung behind to thank Chavez y Chavez for his hospitality, then left out following the trail broken in the snow by the lead party.

They rode mostly in silence for a while, but as they drew up alongside the body of the spotted mule, stiff and swollen now some fifty yards off the trail, Jenny spoke solemnly, "I cried when he shot it, Cal. It had really been faithful, up until the last when it finally balked. It didn't deserve to be killed."

"No," Cal agreed simply, "I don't suppose it did." All along it had been the mule, maybe the main reason Cal had kept thinking he was chasing McGuire rather than Usery.

Now all three of them were dead, along with some others who didn't deserve to die, either. Dead. Just dead.

They caught up to the other party half an hour later, were in Fairview by late afternoon, and made Grafton in a group on tired mounts shortly after dark. The next day the party from Hermosa, led by Lige Martin and Roque Gutierrez, showed up, and late that afternoon there was once again a burial crew scraping away snow and picking and shoveling out a grave in the half-frozen ground at the Grafton cemetery. At two o'clock the body of Quentin Usery, lying in a plain wooden box, was brought forth, and the Reverend Nathan Gregg read Scripture before a very small crowd as the casket was lowered into the ground and covered over. At the head of the grave a marker was placed which, with all of the characteristic brevity of Westerners, simply read:

QUENTIN USERY
Died of Snakebite
November 14, 1886

And a few graves away, an unmarked cross was removed and a marker carrying the name of Guthrie McGuire put in its place. There were no mournful lingerers at either site.

The day following, a froze-out miner from up Magdalena way made application for the job of marshal of Grafton. Cal Sawyer, ignoring the irony of the man's timing, gladly tendered his own resignation as the temporary holder of that position, and a short while later went by the *Myriad*, knowing Jenny would be there. A dance had been scheduled for Saturday night, and he had no intention of ever again being the second man to ask her to one.

Over at the marshal's office, Enos Cooper's bear grease stood as crystal clear as the sky was blue. And, but for miles away on a creosotebush flat where a puffy breeze blew a tiny wisp of snow from the frozen body of the spotted mule, there was no wind at all.

AUTHOR'S NOTE

The places in this novel are real. Socorro County no longer
covers the territory it did then; and Grafton, a little-known
mining town which was in its prime at about the time of the
story, today stands only as a barely traceable ghost of its former self. The author's descriptions of the town and its people are of his own invention, but the mountains and the canyons, the foothills and the flats—the Black Range, the
Cuchillo Negro, the Cañada Alamosa country—are all as
depicted, with only a few liberties taken for the sake of the
story.

Of the other towns mentioned, Fairview (now Winston),
Cuchillo (originally Cuchillo Negro), Monticello, even
Chloride and Kingston, are occupied, undoubtedly by fewer
people, but occupied nonetheless. Hillsboro, which served
early on as the county seat for what became Sierra County,
is a quiet little mountain community, home to perhaps a
hundred people who particularly favor the peaceful life, and
will probably remain that way, unless . . . well, who knows
—another mining boom maybe?

Magdalena and Socorro, ranching and farming communi-
ties respectively, are alive and well with modern futures almost assured. Hermosa, except for its cemetery and what
has been preserved as a part of a modern-day ranch head-
quarters, is, like Grafton, all but gone forever.